In The Sunken Garden

This Armada book belongs to:

____

____

____

Also in this series

1 The Double Disguise

More Kay Tracey Mysteries will be published in Armada

KAY TRACEY

In The Sunken Garden

Frances K. Judd

Published in the U.S.A. in 1978 by
Lamplight Publishing, Inc. and in 1980
by Bantam Books, Inc.
First published in the U.K. in Armada in 1983 by
Fontana Paperbacks, 8 Grafton Street, London W1X 3LA.

Printed and bound in Great Britain by
William Collins Sons & Co. Ltd., Glasgow

Contents

1

Mistaken Identity

"Now let me see. Do I have everything Mum told me to bring home?"

Kay Tracey, a pretty high school girl, spoke the words aloud as she thoughtfully studied her shopping list. Her mother was planning to give a luncheon to a small group of friends that Saturday afternoon and Kay had driven to Carmont to do the shopping.

"No, I knew I had forgotten something!" she exclaimed, checking the list. "Flowers for the table and some decorations."

Directly across the street Kay noticed a florist's shop which had an attractive display in the window. After locking the car she went over to look at it, and then entered the store.

"Good morning," she said to the man in charge. "I should like some flowers for a centrepiece at a luncheon."

"Our roses are beautiful," he suggested. "They came only ten minutes ago from the greenhouse. Let me show them to you."

Quickly he went to a rear room where many of the flowers were kept. Scarcely had he disappeared when the shop door opened and a tall young man in a grey suit came hurrying into the building. He glanced toward Kay and stopped abruptly.

"Well, hello," he greeted her cheerfully. "I certainly didn't expect to see you up so bright and early! Great party last night, wasn't it?"

Kay was taken completely by surprise since she had never seen the man before and she hadn't been to a party the previous evening. She had remained at home in nearby Brantwood with her mother and her cousin, Bill Tracey, a young lawyer who had lived with the Traceys since the death of Kay's father.

Before she could say that she thought the man must have mistaken her for another person, he glanced impatiently about the shop.

"The manager isn't around? Well, I can't wait. I'm in a big hurry. See you again soon."

Waving to Kay, he went out the door and started across the street. Before he was out of sight, the florist returned with a large bouquet of pink and white roses.

"Didn't I hear someone enter the shop?" he asked Kay.

"Yes, it was that man who is crossing the street now." Moving to the window, she pointed to the stranger. "Do you know him?"

The florist shook his head. "He isn't one of my regular customers. I don't remember ever having seen him before."

"It was strange," Kay remarked, half to herself. "The young man evidently mistook me for somebody he knew. I didn't think anyone in the world looked like me, certainly not in Brantwood!"

She turned her attention to the roses, finally bought a dozen and a half, and left the shop.

"Now I'll get some decorations and then my shopping will be finished," she thought as she carried the box to the car.

As the nearest store where cards and decorations could be bought was two blocks away, Kay decided it would be quicker to drive there than to walk. At the first corner she was held up by a red traffic light. While waiting for it to change, she noticed two girls on the sidewalk. Catching a glimpse of Kay, they began to wave and call to her.

"Say, where did you borrow that good-looking car?" one asked cheerfully. "Give us a lift!"

Kay glanced over her shoulder, half expecting to see that another automobile had drawn up behind her own. Her car was the only one for some distance down the street. Obviously the two girls were calling to her, under the impression that they were friends.

"I never saw either of them before in my life," thought Kay in dismay. "How weird. This makes the second time in fifteen minutes that I've been mistaken for another person!"

The traffic light changed to green so she drove on before the two girls could reach her. A moment later she thought regretfully, "I wish I had waited and asked them the name of my double. Well, the chance is gone now."

While she shopped for some pretty decorations, Kay continued to think about the incident. So deeply absorbed was she that she didn't see a girl named Chris Eaton enter the shop. The two attended the same high school at Carmont, commuting each day from their homes in Brantwood. Chris was not a popular student, and although Kay tried to be friendly, she was regarded with jealousy and envy by the Eaton girl.

"Oh, hello, Kay," said Chris. "What are you doing here?"

"Good morning, Chris. I'm just buying some decorations for my mother. She's giving a little luncheon this afternoon."

"Really?" Chris's tone became bragging. "My mother doesn't bother about *little luncheons*. I suppose you heard that she is giving a wonderful dinner party this week for Monsieur and Madame Le Blanc."

"No, Chris, I hadn't heard," Kay responded drily.

"We'll have at least forty guests. Monsieur and Madame Le Blanc are such distinguished persons."

"I've never heard of them."

"Probably not," Chris returned, walking away. "They came from Europe recently and we'll be the first to entertain them."

Kay made her purchase and left the shop, not in the least disturbed by Chris Eaton's remarks. As she approached her car she noticed a beautiful collie dog sitting at the curb. He sprang up, barking joyously, and tried to get into the automobile as she opened the door.

"No, you can't come with me," Kay commanded sternly. "Go back to your owner!"

She drove away slowly. Glancing back, she was disturbed to see that the dog had followed the car. As she drove faster he was hard pressed to keep the automobile within view.

"Poor thing," she thought. "I wonder if *he* is mistaking me for someone else, too."

Stopping the car, she again tried to send the dog away. Finally he trotted off down the street. Satisfied that she had seen the last of him, Kay continued toward home, making frequent stops for traffic lights.

Halfway to Brantwood she glanced into the side mirror and was dismayed to see that the friendly animal was once more directly behind her. His tongue was hanging out and he limped as he ran.

"Why, the poor thing is exhausted," the girl thought, stopping the car. "I can't let this go on."

When she opened the car door the dog crawled in and licked her hand with his tongue. Lifting him to the seat beside her, she patted his head.

"I'll take you home with me," she decided sympathetically. "I guess I'll keep you until I can find your owner."

At the Tracey house a few minutes later Kay began to unload packages from the rear of the car. To her astonishment the beautiful dog seized one of the parcels in his teeth and carried it proudly to the front porch. Carefully placing it on the steps he returned for a second package.

"So I have a helper!" laughed Kay, delighted by the trick. "Someone must have trained you well."

As the animal started across the garden with a box of rolls which he held by the string, another dog, long a neighbourhood pest, made a sudden dart at him. The attack was brief but vicious. As the two animals nipped at each other, the carton from the bakery was torn open. Before Kay could prevent it the rolls tumbled out on the ground. Seizing one in his mouth, the attacking dog retreated to his own front porch.

"Oh, dear, all that food ruined," Kay murmured, picking up the remains from the dirt. "It's lucky I bought twice as many as Mother had on her list."

Upon being introduced to the new dog, Mrs Tracey looked at him doubtfully. However, she was so busy with plans for the luncheon that she quickly agreed Kay could keep the dog until the owner could be located.

"It's strange how he followed me home—just as if he knew me," Kay remarked thoughtfully.

"Yes," agreed her mother, "but dogs are the least of my concern right now. I have about a hundred things to do before one o'clock!"

"I'll take care of fifty of them for you," Kay laughed as she helped put away the various parcels. "I noticed that the front porch needs sweeping. I'll start in there."

While the girl was busy with her task, Ronald Earle, a young man who considered Kay by far the most attractive person in Brantwood, drove by in his car. He stopped to talk for a few minutes and asked her to go for a ride.

"I wish I could," said Kay, "but I've promised to help Mother with a luncheon."

After he had gone, Kay went to the kitchen to prepare a salad. While cutting up some fruit, the sharp knife with which she was working slipped and Kay cut her hand.

"Oh, no," she sighed, as she let the cold water run over the wound, which would not stop bleeding. "I guess I'll have to put on a bandage."

This she did, but it got in her way and things were barely ready when the guests began to arrive for the luncheon.

Kay knew all of them well. Several of her mother's friends asked about her injured hand. One wanted to know if she had been in an automobile accident! Another blamed it on a possible mishap in connection with the girl's work as an amateur detective.

"I seem to be involved in another mystery right now," Kay laughed. "This morning two persons mistook me for another girl. And even a stray dog adopted me as his owner. I must have a double, although I certainly haven't seen her yet."

After lunch Kay decided to take the dog for a walk along the river. Both of them enjoyed it and Kay became more attached to the animal every moment. He was not only lovable, but very intelligent. "I'll hate to let you go," she said, patting him affectionately.

Returning home late in the afternoon, she was about to enter the house, when Ronald's car again stopped at the curb.

"Hey, thanks for nothing!" he shouted angrily.

"What did I do now?" asked Kay, turning and walking toward the car.

"Didn't you tell me you had to help your mother with a luncheon?"

"Yes, I did, Ronald. But while the women were busy afterwards I slipped out for a litle walk with my new dog."

"You're sure you *walked*?"

"Of course! Why?"

"I though I saw you riding with a young man about ten minutes ago. He had a maroon car."

"I don't know any young men who own maroon cars, Ronald. You were wrong."

"Guess I must have been," he answered with relief.

"Three other people have mistaken me for someone else today, Ronald. Tell me, what did this other girl look like?"

"Why, just like you, Kay, only now that I think of it, she was wearing a blue dress and yours is white. She might have been a year or two older."

"I wish I could see her, Ronald. It's fascinating—suddenly I'm a twin!"

After Ronald left, Kay again joined her mother's friends.

The afternoon drew pleasantly to a close. Nearly all the guests had left the house when Bill Tracey's car pulled into the driveway. The young lawyer ran across the lawn, came up the front porch steps two at a time and burst into the living room.

"I'm sorry to break up the party this way," he apologized, "but I have terrible news!" Suddenly he saw Kay, who stood across the room, and he stopped abruptly. "Why, it's you!" he said.

"Of course," she replied in astonishment. "Did you think I might be some other girl."

Bill Tracey was in no mood for joking. Rushing across the room, he clasped his cousin in his arms.

"Kay, you're really safe!" he exclaimed in an unsteady voice. "Thank goodness, it wasn't you after all!"

2

Complications

"Bill, did you think Kay had been injured?" asked Mrs Tracey before her daughter could speak.

"Yes, I did," the young lawyer answered seriously. "Doctor Brown called me from the hosptial about ten minutes ago. He had just treated an unconscious girl who was injured in an automobile accident."

"And he thought she was Kay?" asked the girl's mother.

"He seemed to have no doubt of it. That was what gave me such a shock when I saw her here. I came home to get you before driving on to the hospital."

"Doctor Brown knows me fairly well," Kay remarked slowly. "If he was fooled, then this other girl must be practically a walking picture of me."

"Kay thinks she has a mysterious double," explained Mrs Tracey. "Several times today she was mistaken for someone else."

"I wish I could see her for myself," declared her daughter.

It was evident that the incident had left Bill Tracey somewhat upset. Offering an apology to the few remaining guests, he went quickly to his room.

Soon all the guests left the house except a Mrs Graham who was waiting for a taxi. When the cab did not come, Kay offered to take the woman home in her car.

"Oh, I shouldn't trouble you," Mrs Graham protested.

"I'd really like to do it," replied Kay eagerly.

Since the woman lived only two blocks from the hospital, Kay thought that she could visit her mysterious double on the way back. Telling her mother that she might be a litle late in returning, Kay took the guest home, then stopped at the hospital.

She was disappointed to find out that the patient who bore such a remarkable resemblance to herself had been discharged. After regaining consciousness and being treated for a sprained ankle, the girl had refused to remain longer, disregarding the advice of doctors.

"Can you tell me her name?" inquired Kay thoughtfully.

The young woman in charge of the desk glanced through a card index file.

"Yes, her name is Jane Barton."

"And her address?"

"1500 Sunset Drive."

"Thank you very much," Kay responded as she turned away.

It was disappointing to have missed meeting the patient, and Kay wondered if it would be worth her while to look for the girl at the Sunset Drive address.

Kay loved being involved in a mystery. With the help of her best friends the Worth twins, Betty and Wendy, the sixteen-year-old girl had solved many cases in and around her home town. As a result, Kay had a wide reputation as an amateur detective and many people came to her for advice.

But now, Kay thought, tucking in a curly stray wisp of her chestnut-brown hair, she had bumped straight into a new kind of mystery. Never before had she been mistaken for anybody else. True, it had seemed funny at first, but now Kay felt she had to untangle this mystery quickly.

"I'll just call Jane Barton's home and ask if she's getting along all right," she told herself now as she returned to her car.

Although she searched carefully through the Bs in the directory, Kay could not find a family by the name of Barton listed as living on Sunset Drive.

"That's strange," she thought as she went back to the car. "I wonder if the girl could be living with a family of a different name? I'm sure I have the address right—1500 Sunset Drive."

Now that Kay's interest had been stimulated she decided to drive out to the house the first chance she got. It was too late to make the trip this afternoon, for no doubt dinner would be waiting by the time she would get home. Turning into the Tracey driveway a few minutes later, she was met at the side door by her mother.

"A man who calls himself Joe Craken is in the living room waiting for you, Kay. He won't tell me why he wishes to see you, but from his general attitude I think he means to make trouble."

"Craken—I don't know anyone by that name." "He is a very rough-looking fellow. Bill went back to his office. Then his secretary called to say he had to go out of town. I'm rather worried."

"I'll see what he wants, Mother. That will be the quickest way to get rid of him."

As Kay entered the living room, a short, stout man with a disfiguring scar on his right cheek arose from the couch. He quickly looked Kay up and down.

"I'll be brief and to the point, Miss Tracey. You owe me the price of a new car and something extra for personal injuries."

"I owe *you!*" exclaimed Kay incredulously. "Why, I don't even know who you are!"

"Now don't pull that stuff. It won't get you anywhere. You thought I didn't know who you were but the police learned your name."

"Perhaps you have mistaken me for another person."

"You're Kay Tracey, aren't you?"

"Yes."

"Well, that was the name the police gave me. You're the one I'm after."

"Why do you think I owe you so much money?"

"Listen!" the man said unpleasantly. "It won't get you any place pretending not to know anything about the accident. You smashed my car and injured one of my passengers."

"Your claim is ridiculous!" exclaimed Mrs Tracey before Kay could reply. "My daughter has not been in an automobile accident."

"She probably didn't tell you about it, Ma'am," retorted Mr Craken bluntly. "Look at her hand all bandaged up. And I found out the car she was driving belonged to a man who is in Europe. So she must have stolen it."

"You've mistaken me for another girl," Kay said coldly, "and apparently the police have too."

"So you're trying to make me believe that some other girl looks just like you?"

"It happens to be the truth, Mr Craken. I found out today that evidently I have a double."

"Are you giving me a straight story?"

"My daughter is not in the habit of telling lies," said Mrs Tracey indignantly.

"No offence meant," the man returned quickly. "If I made a mistake it's because the police gave me the wrong name. Who is this other girl?"

Annoyed by the visitor's rudeness, Kay made up her mind that she would not disclose the identity of her "twin" until she had made some investigation of the case. She did promise Mr Craken that if she should meet the girl she would try to find out something for him. With this assurance the man was forced to leave.

While Kay was telling her mother what she had learned at the hospital, Wendy and Betty Worth stopped at the house on their way home from the theatre. They too learned the entire story.

"Well, if that isn't funny!" cried Betty, the blue-eyed sister. "Wendy and I really are twins, yet we don't look the least bit alike."

"And Kay has a double who isn't even a relative!" added Wendy, laughing.

In appearance as well as in character these sisters were very different. Wendy was tall and dark, very studious, and inclined to be serious. Each week she spent many hours reading and writing poetry, and once she even won a prize for her work.

"I'd like to see my 'twin'," Kay told her friends. "Isn't Sunset Drive located in the western section of the city?"

"Yes, but the street is a long one," replied Betty. "It extends far into the country—six or seven miles at least."

"Oh, yes, I remember the street now," nodded Kay. "Aren't there a number of old estates out that way?"

"Yes, and several real estate developments. It is the oldest part of Brantwood, you know, and at one time was considered very exclusive."

"Perhaps I can convince Ronald to drive me out that way tonight," Kay remarked as her friends arose to leave. "We have a date later."

"I guess Ronald will do just about anything you suggest," Betty said teasingly. "Well, if you run into another mystery, don't forget to count Wendy and me in on it!"

Shortly after eight o'clock Ronald arrived at the Tracey home. He assured Kay that the Sunset Drive route would not be in the least out of their way in going toward the concert they were going to.

"Do you know anyone living on that street?" he asked curiously.

"No," laughed Kay as he helped her into the car, "but I hope soon to meet my mysterious double. I found out that she lives at 1500 Sunset Drive. Where do you think that is?"

"Oh, a long distance out. Probably six miles."

As the car sped along the wide, curving street, Kay looked at the dark old mansions with interest. Many had been abandoned, some were being used as offices and clubhouses, while others had been torn down to make way for modern dwellings.

"I wonder if any of the original families still live on Sunset Drive?" Kay mused, turning her head to gaze back at a particularly elegant old house.

"I guess there are a few families left, but not many. Did you notice the house we just passed?"

"Yes, it was unusually interesting, I thought."

"That was the old Huntley place, Kay. No one has lived there for many years."

"I saw a light in the front window," Kay said quickly.

"You did? Then a family must have moved in very recently. The place has been difficult to rent on account of the mystery connected with it."

"Mystery?" Kay asked excitedly.

"Maybe that isn't the right word to use. I guess I never told you about the Huntleys being distantly related to my family."

"No, Ronald, I never heard you mention them before."

"The truth is, we're not very proud of the relationship," the young man admitted reluctantly. "One of the Huntleys disappeared with some money and has never been traced. At least that's the story. The house has been empty ever since."

Kay wanted to ask Ronald additional questions about the Huntleys but she sensed that he really didn't want to talk about it.

The concert was very good and Kay and Ronald spent an enjoyable evening listening to an excellent band. During an intermission the audience was entertained by a special dance number presented by a talented young woman. Although Kay and Ronald didn't hear her name, they heard the announcer say that the dancer would appear in only one local performance as she had been signed for a show to open in New York City very shortly.

At the conclusion of the last encore, which received many rounds of applause, the young woman turned directly towards Kay. She waved and smiled, then ran gracefully from the floor.

"Do you know her?" Ronald asked in surprise.

Kay shook her head. "I never saw her before in my life."

"She certainly acted as if she were acquainted with you."

"Maybe she's a friend of my double," Kay laughed. The next instant she became serious. "Do you mind waiting here for a minute, Ronald? I'm going to go into the dressing room and talk to that girl. I am curious to find out if she knows me or only thinks she does."

By the time Kay reached the dressing room she discovered that the dancer no longer was there. An attendant explained that the young woman had slipped a coat over her costume and had driven away in a car.

Disappointed, Kay rejoined Ronald and in a short while they started back to Brantwood. As they rolled smoothly along Sunset Drive with the car windows open, they noticed that nearly all the old mansions were in darkness.

"I may have been mistaken about the Huntley place having a light on," Kay said thoughtfully, "but I don't think so."

Soon they drew near the old estate and Ronald stopped the car. "The place looks deserted now," he remarked, staring towards the house. "No sign of a—"

As he spoke, a shrill scream broke the stillness of the night. Ronald and Kay gazed at each other in surprise. Unmistakably the cry had come from the grounds of the Huntley estate!

3

A Cry in the Night

Parking the car at the side of the road, Ronald and Kay ran towards the dark house which was set far back among tall trees. When they reached the front porch they stood still for a moment to listen.

"I don't hear anything now," declared the girl, "but the scream certainly came from this house."

"Yes, it did," agreed Ronald, turning the beam of his flashlight on the lower windows. "It sounded like someone being hurt."

"We might knock on the door," Kay suggested uncertainly.

Before Ronald could reply, an upstairs window was flung wide open. A man, whose face could not be seen clearly from below, peered down at them.

"What's going on?" he demanded suspiciously. "Why do you come here?"

"While we were driving past we heard someone scream," explained Ronald. "We thought the cry came from this house."

"No one make noise here until you come prowling around! My wife and I are trying to sleep. Go now or I call ze police."

"We're only trying to be helpful," Kay protested quickly.

"You hear me?" shouted the man wrathfully. "Go away or I telephone ze police!"

Kay and Ronald went back to the car and drove to Brantwood. They were sure they had heard a cry, and they decided that the unpleasant foreign man must have been quarrelling with is wife.

The following afternoon, accompanied by Wendy and Betty, Kay again went to the Sunset Drive district. For several blocks the numbers ran evenly on the houses, then suddenly the girls realized that many of the old mansions had no address. Although they asked at several places they were unable to locate a house listed as number 1500. From a woman who lived near the Huntley estate the girls did learn that a man and his wife by the name of Le Blanc had moved in there during the past week.

"Le Blanc," the girl said to her chums. "Chris Eaton told me her parents are having a party for a Monsieur and Madame Le Blanc. I wonder if they are the same people?"

"It would be just like Chris's mother to make friends with strangers if she thought they had either position or money," remarked Betty. "Mrs Eaton is a social climber."

"Despite her wealth she never succeeded in climbing very far!" laughed Wendy. "I know our parents are relieved that Mrs Eaton didn't invite them to her so-called grand dinner."

After dropping off her friends, Kay drove home. She happened to pass Doctor Brown's office and decided impulsively to stop and talk to him.

"Now let me look closely at you, young lady," the man laughed jovially. "Is this Kay Tracey or Jane Barton?"

"Are we really so much alike, Doctor?"

"Yes, your resemblance to Jane Barton is astounding. Yesterday I was fooled completely."

"Are you sure you know who I am now?" Kay asked with a smile.

"As long as Jane Barton has a bandaged foot I'll have no trouble in identifying you," replied the doctor. "By the way, she was here only a few minutes ago."

"Really? How is she getting along now?"

"Oh, as well as can be expected, but she is impatient. She didn't like it when I told her she shouldn't use her foot for several days. That girl has a will of her own and a temper!"

"I wish I could have met her," Kay remarked regretfully.

"The next time she comes in to have her foot bandaged I'll call you," offered the doctor. "I would enjoy seeing you two together. I've never seen two people who look more alike."

Kay had no chance to think about Jane Barton the following day for, as usual, school activities took up her time. With Betty, Wendy and other members of a newly organized dance club, she stayed late at school to practise new steps with Miss Grover, the instructor. Chris Eaton, although she hadn't been invited to join the dance club, lingered to watch the girls go through a hard drill.

"Aren't you afraid you'll trip and fall?" she asked Kay disdainfully. "You certainly swing your feet around awkwardly!"

Kay refused to become annoyed and did not even reply.

"I'd never waste time studying dancing under an inferior teacher," Chris went on scornfully. "My parents are going to have me take lessons from a wonderful person."

Her words might have angered Kay but she knew that Miss Grover was perhaps the best dance teacher in Carmont. The girls were thrilled when she praised the club for the progress it had made.

"Kay has done especially well," the teacher declared proudly, "and for that reason I'm making her the leader of our routines."

She announced that the group would perform at a benefit show to be held soon for the Children's Home. Annoyed at this news, Chris picked up her school books and left the gymnasium.

Kay and the twins took showers and changed into street clothes. Then they rushed to the railway station to catch their train home. Not until the girls were in the train did Kay notice that she was carrying an extra textbook.

"Why, this isn't my history book," she exclaimed in surprise. "I wonder where I picked it up?"

Opening the cover she saw Chris Eaton's name, and groaned.

"I would have to carry away *her* book! Now she'll probably say that I kept it on purpose."

"Give it to her in the morning," suggested Betty carelessly.

"She probably intended to study this evening," Kay replied, shaking her head. "No, I'll have to take it to her house tonight, even if it is annoying."

The Traceys usually had dinner at six o'clock. Right after dinner Kay took the textbook to Chris's home. Not until she was at the door did it occur to her that this evening was the one which had been set for Mrs Eaton's so-called "grand party."

"I've probably arrived at an awkward hour," the Tracey girl told herself, "but I don't have to go inside."

When the door was opened by a butler she gave him the book, explaining how the mix-up had occurred.

"I will tell Miss Eaton you are here," the servant said politely.

"No, please don't bother," Kay protested, but the butler had turned away leaving the door half open.

From within the house could be heard the sound of laughter and music. Evidently many of the guests had arrived. As Kay waited uncomfortably, a man in evening clothes, his reddish hair combed in wisps over a bald head, appeared in the hallway.

He stopped abruptly as he saw Kay, staring hard at her. With a quick glance about the halls to make certain that no one else was near, he moved straight towards the door.

"You are to return immediately to ze house, Mademoiselle," he ordered sharply. "You were not invited to ze dinner. No! Go quickly, pleese!"

For an instant Kay could not identify the man. Then she recognized his voice. Only the previous evening he had ordered her away from the Huntley mansion, and now he arrogantly was telling her to leave the Eaton premises! Unquestionably he must be Monsieur Le Blanc, the guest of honour whom the Eatons thought was so distinguished.

"You hear me?" the man demanded. "Go quickly. *Oui!*"

"Oh, I'm not intruding," Kay responded, more amused than annoyed.

Without waiting for the butler to return, she walked quickly away. Before she had gone far she regretted that she hadn't stayed to talk a few more minutes longer with the weird stranger.

"Now that I think of it, I wonder why he spoke to me so abruptly?" she mused. "He acted as if he knew me well and that it was his right to give me orders."

Suddenly Kay realized that Monsieur Le Blanc might have mistaken her for Jane Barton. If that was the case it was very likely that the man knew where her double lived. Maybe she even lived in his own house!

"This business of having a twin becomes more interesting every minute," she thought. "I really must find Jane Barton and have a talk with her."

When Kay got home she looked in the evening newspaper. She had placed an ad in the lost and found column describing the dog which had followed her home.

"I almost hope nobody answers," she thought, reading over the ad. "I'd really love to keep him and call him Jerry."

The next morning Kay was at home when the postman arrived with several pieces of mail.

"A registered letter for you, Miss Tracey," he said, offering her a paper to sign.

"I suppose it's an answer to that ad about Jerry," Kay thought, glancing at the long envelope which the postman placed in her hand.

To her surprise she saw that it had the name of a law firm on it, Duster and Trout at Ottenville. Wondering what it might be, Kay ripped open the envelope. One glance at the typewritten letter told her that she was in serious trouble.

In concise legal terminology the firm of Duster and Trout informed her that they represented Joe Craken and they were instituting a suit against her. She was accused of wrecking Mr Craken's car while driving a stolen automobile. Also, she would have to pay for injuries to a passenger in the Craken car. The letter ended by saying that witnesses were available who would swear in court to all of the facts as stated.

"This is outrageous!" Kay cried, running into the house.

"What's wrong?" asked Mrs Tracey when she saw her daughter's face.

"Just read this letter, Mother."

Mrs Tracey quickly scanned the paper. "Oh, dear, this is serious," she said anxiously.

"It might be serious," agreed Kay in a grim voice, "but I'm sure Bill will know how to prove that I had nothing to do with the accident. I'll just turn this over to him."

Mrs Tracey's look of anxiety deepened. "Bill is out of town," she said despairingly. "He left unexpectedly Saturday evening. He didn't tell us where to reach him. Now what are we going to do?"

4

An Abandoned Garden

"Bill's absence does complicate things," Kay agreed. "But the case can't reach court for a while anyway."

"We'll have plenty of time to prepare a defence," agreed her mother. "It's foolish to worry. Bill will return in a day or two, and he'll straighten out everything."

Kay put the letter away. "I'll forget about it for now. I'd better hurry or I'll be late for school."

Kay picked up her books and ran nearly all the way to the railway station. She arrived just as the train was about to pull out and swung aboard the last car. She was breathless as she sank into a seat opposite the Worth twins.

"One of these mornings you'll sleep a minute too long," Wendy laughed.

Kay explained why she had been late, asking the twins not to tell anyone about the letter.

"You've probably been mistaken for that double of yours again!" exclaimed Betty.

"I don't know what to think. I thought I had convinced Mr Craken that I had nothing to do with the accident. But after he left me he went to this Ottenville law firm. At first he didn't say I was responsible for injury to a passenger."

"It looks to me as if the lawyers are trying to build up a big case out of nothing," Wendy said indignantly.

Kay nodded her head. "I think so too. I'm sure Bill will get me out of it somehow, but I feel sorry for Jane Barton."

"For all we know, the accident may have been Mr Craken's fault," added Betty.

"I wish I could talk with the girl," said Kay. "I've been wondering if she lives at the old Huntley house with Monsieur Le Blanc and his wife."

"With whom?" demanded Betty, suddenly alert.

"Monsieur Le Blanc. I found out last night that he and his wife have rented the Huntley place. And when I went to the Eaton house to take back Chris's book he very arrogantly ordered me away!"

Wendy and Betty listened eagerly to Kay's story, and then told her that according to neighbourhood gossip the Eaton party had been a big failure. Monsieur Le Blanc and his wife had boasted outrageously of their ability as dancing instructors, and had bored all the guests.

"So Monsieur Le Blanc is a dancing teacher," Kay laughed. "From the way Chris acted I thought that he must have descended from royalty at least."

"Sh!" Wendy whispered. "Here she comes now."

Chris walked slowly down the aisle, pausing as she reached the section where Kay and the twins were sitting.

"Oh, thanks for bringing over the book last night, Kay. I'm so tired this morning," she said with a yawn. "I didn't get to bed until after one o'clock. What a party! Monsieur Le Blanc is such a fascinating person!"

Hoping to get a little information from the girl, Kay remarked that she had heard the Le Blancs had rented the old Huntley house. "I'm surprised they need such a large place. There are only the two of them, aren't there?"

"Why don't you ask Monsieur Le Blanc?" Chris replied with a mysterious air. "I am sure he wouldn't want me to discuss his affairs."

Feeling that she had scored against her rival, the girl walked on down the aisle.

"I can guess why the Le Blancs rented the Huntley house," Kay told the twins. "They probably intend to use it for a dance studio."

"Why do you think Jane Barton may be living with them?" Betty asked curiously.

"Because of the way Monsieur Le Blanc told me to leave the Eaton house last night."

"You think he mistook you for Jane Barton?"

"Yes. After school let's go out there and see what we can find out."

"We'd love to do it," Wendy said eagerly, "but don't you think he would remember you?"

"Maybe I could disguise myself," answered Kay. "I'll borrow some of Mother's clothes and put on make-up."

Five o'clock found the girls standing on the front porch of the Huntley house. Kay wore a large hat which came far down over her forehead, but even so Wendy and Betty were afraid she might be identified.

"What will you say to Monsieur Le Blanc?" Wendy whispered nervously.

"I'll play it by ear," returned Kay, as she rang the doorbell.

A moment later the wife of the dancing master came to the door. She was a tall, thin woman with dark hair and eyes. Ten years before she might have been beautiful, but now hard lines surrounded her mouth, and her eyes were cold and unfriendly.

"Monsieur Le Blanc is very busy now," she said, speaking with an accent. "There will be no more auditions today."

"Oh, we just wanted to welcome—" Kay began.

Before she could finish, the man appeared in the doorway. He didn't recognize Kay but he exclaimed angrily, "Always someone at the door!" Running his hands through his hair with a nervous gesture, he added. "Never have I ze moment of peace in zis *chateau*. All day ze stupid girls annoy me for try-outs, because I am ze great *maitre de danse!*"

"Now, Henri," protested his wife soothingly, "these young ladies say they did not come here for a try-out."

Monsieur Le Blanc ignored her and music began to play somewhere in the house.

"There, ze dance begins now!" he cried, turning away. "I must go! Do not bother me with visitors."

"My husband is temperamental as are all great artists," Madame Le Blanc said with an apologetic sigh. "You will excuse it, please?"

"Oh, yes, we quite understand," replied Kay. "We'll just come inside and wait until the rehearsals are over."

"My husband would not like that," Madame Le Blanc said, frowning. "The rehearsal will last many hours. I also must be excused for Monsieur expects me to help him."

Gently but firmly the woman closed the door in the girls' faces.

"A lot we learned!" Betty said in disappointment.

"What do you think is going on in there anyway?" Wendy asked, looking towards the upstairs windows.

"I intend to find out," Kay announced grimly. "We'll get into the house somehow."

"I'm not going to crawl in any windows," Wendy announced.

"Oh, we'll find a perfectly legal way to enter," laughed Kay. "Let's try the back door. Perhaps a servant will let us in."

Walking around the house, the girls knocked on both the side and back doors, but no one answered. As they were turning away, Kay noticed a sunken garden with steps down to the river at the far end of the Huntley estate. The entire place was overgrown with weeds, and the shrubbery had not been clipped and there was a broken-down gazebo in the centre.

"This must have been a beautiful garden," Kay remarked as the girls wandered along one of the paths. "Too bad it's been neglected."

After crossing over a small arched bridge, they sat down on a stone bench. Nearby, on a slightly tilted pedestal, stood a crystal ball.

"Why don't you tell our fortunes, Wendy," Betty said jokingly.

Wendy walked over to the crystal ball and gazed into it.

"What do you see in the crystal ball? Just tell our fortunes," Betty asked with a laugh.

"Not a thing except my own nose!" Wendy laughed. She straightened up and walked back to the porch. "Shall we go to the car now?"

"You and Betty go ahead, I'll join you in a minute," Kay said quickly.

"What are you going to do?" demanded Betty. "I bet you've thought up a way to get into the house!"

"I'm just going to try the back door again."

"Okay, Betty and I will wait in the car," Wendy said, turning away.

After her friends had disappeared around the corner of the house, Kay went to the back door. She knocked several times but no one came. Just as she was turning away, the door was suddenly opened by a girl wearing ballet slippers and a dancing costume.

"Can I help you?"

"Yes, I'd like to see Jane Barton, please," Kay requested boldly.

"Jane Barton?" the girl repeated, shaking her head. "There's no one here by that name."

"She was in a car accident."

"You must have the wrong house." The girl closed the door quickly, but not before Kay had seen the look of panic on her face.

"I bet she knew whom I meant," Kay thought as she walked slowly toward the road. "Strange things are going on in that house."

Wendy and Betty, waiting in the car, stared at Kay.

"How did you manage to change your clothes so quickly?" Betty asked half accusingly. "And you told us you had no scheme for getting inside the house."

"What are you talking about," protested Kay. "These clothes are the ones I've worn ever since we came here."

"But we saw you just a minute ago in a different dress," insisted Betty. "You were carrying a basket. Or could it have been—"

"My double!" finished Kay, her voice tense with excitement. "Which way did she go?"

5

A Puzzling Paper

"We saw the girl walking towards the sunken garden," said Betty. "She looked exactly like you!"

"We've got to find her!" cried Kay as she ran back to the house.

The Worth twins rushed out of the car and followed their friend. When they reached the sunken garden there was no sign of the girl.

"She isn't here now," observed Kay in disappointment.

"She was at this very spot only a few seconds ago," insisted Wendy.

"There's her basket!" exclaimed Betty pointing towards the gazebo.

"Maybe she'll be back in a minute or two," declared Kay. "We'll wait for her."

The lunch basket had been left on a wooden bench, but no one could be seen in the garden or anywhere on the grounds. Kay and the twins sat down to wait. Time passed but the girl did not return. It was rapidly growing dark. Finally Wendy glanced uneasily at her watch.

"It's almost dinner time. Betty and I should be home in a little while or Mother will get worried."

Disappointed, Kay stood up. "I guess it's useless to wait any longer. We may as well go."

"It's certainly strange the way she disappeared," Betty remarked as the three slowly walked back to the car. "Maybe she saw us waiting for her and deliberately stayed away."

"I was thinking the same thing," admitted Kay. "Still, she has no good reason for wanting to avoid me—at least not that I know of."

Kay couldn't stop thinking about the whole situation and later that evening she finally decided to do something. Knowing that Chris would probably be at the library, she went to the Eaton home to talk to Chris's mother. Kay directed the conversation, encouraging the woman to talk about the guests she had had for dinner recently.

"I really don't know the Le Blancs well at all," Mrs Eaton confessed reluctantly.

"I guess you met them through friends?"

"Well, no, I didn't. Chris told me about them. Somehow she found out the man was a famous dancer in Europe. I really entertained the couple because Chris was so eager for me to do it."

"Do the Le Blancs have a girl living with them?"

"I don't know. Madame Le Blanc mentioned that they had taken the old Huntley house, but she didn't say whether or not they have children." Mrs Eaton frowned thoughtfully. "Chris has been pleading with me to be allowed to take dancing lessons from Monsieur, but I don't think I'll let her."

"You don't think that the man is as talented as he says?" asked Kay.

"Oh, undoubtedly he is a famous dancing teacher," Mrs Eaton returned quickly. "But he's very strange. And his lessons are expensive."

"Is he going to use the old Huntley house for a studio?"

"I don't know," replied Mrs Eaton.

The woman became reluctant to answer any more questions, so Kay changed the subject and soon left the house. Back home a few minutes later, she noticed that Bill's half of the double garage remained empty.

"Not here yet," she thought uneasily. "I was sure he would get back tonight."

Mrs Tracey was even more disturbed than her daughter over the young lawyer's prolonged absence. Without telling Kay, she had sent telegrams to various out-of-town hotels where she thought he might be staying, but no answer had come.

Kay tried not to worry about the lawsuit, but she was finding it increasingly difficult to keep her mind on her school work.

After school, members of the dancing club gathered in the auditorium to practise for the benefit show. Kay was one of the first to arrive. While waiting for the other girls to change into their costumes, she stood at the window watching the dark clouds in the sky.

"I think there's going to be a bad storm," she remarked to Wendy. "Do you think we should cut practice and hurry to the station?"

"Oh, it probably will be a quick shower," answered Wendy. "Anyway, I brought my umbrella."

When Miss Grover entered the auditorium, Kay asked her if she knew Brantwood's new dancing teacher, Monsieur Le Blanc.

"No, I can't claim the honour."

"You aren't familiar with his name?"

"No, I must admit that Le Blanc is a blank to me," laughed the young woman.

As the girls rehearsed, the room gradually became dark. Miss Grover turned on the lights, so no one noticed the change in the weather.

Suddenly everyone in the room was startled by a vivid flash of lightning. At the same moment the electricity went off. The girls screamed with fright.

"Now, girls, this is nothing," said Miss Grover calmly. "Just a little storm. In a moment the lights will go on again. Then we shall resume—"

Her words trailed away as the wind shook the building

and rattled the windows. Outside the trees bent back and forth crazily.

Suddenly a heavy object crashed through the skylight of the auditorium. Acting instinctively Kay threw herself against Betty who stood directly beneath the splintered glass. As she pushed her out of the way, a large chunk of wood fell to the floor, barely missing both girls.

"Oh!" gasped Betty, staring at the wood. "If that thing had hit me on the head I might have been killed! You saved my life!"

The other girls gathered around Kay, and in spite of her protests that "it was nothing", insisted that she was a heroine. She was relieved when Miss Grover, alarmed by the intensity of the storm, urged the dancers to go quickly to the dressing room.

"The storm seems to be increasing in violence," she declared nervously. "It isn't safe here."

While the girls were changing their clothes, the lights came on again. Soon Kay and the twins were ready to leave the building. They found many students gathered at the exit, afraid to brave the raging wind.

"What should we do, Kay?" asked Wendy as the girls stood at the door.

"The wind may not die down for a while. If we wait here very long we'll miss our train."

"Oh, I think we can get to the station," declared Betty confidently.

"Let's try it," urged Kay, buttoning her coat up around her neck.

With heads bent low, the girls started away from the school grounds. The wind was even stronger than they had thought. Dust was blown into their eyes. Betty's hat was whipped from her head, and Kay had difficulty in holding on to her books and papers. At last they reached the station, rather exhausted from the battle.

"The storm surely will have passed over by the time we get home," Wendy said hopefully.

When the train pulled into the Brantwood station the girls found that the wind was blowing harder than before.

"It's silly to try to walk home in this," declared Kay. "Let's take a cab."

They summoned a taxi and with sighs of relief settled themselves for a comfortable ride. After Wendy and Betty got out at their home, Kay went on alone. As the cab neared her house, the girl began to gather up her books and papers. Suddenly she noticed a folded yellow sheet lying on the seat.

"That doesn't belong to me," Kay thought, picking it up.

She knew Wendy and Betty hadn't brought any papers home with them from school. Very likely the sheet had been left in the taxi by a passenger.

Curious, Kay unfolded it to see if it had any value. Her eye fell upon a long, typewritten list of names. After each appeared a capital letter, W, P, or M printed with a pencil.

"I wonder if this is some sort of mailing list?" Kay said to herself.

She was about to hand the paper to the cab driver when a name suddenly stood out on the sheet. It was her own, Kay Tracey!

After the name had been written a designating letter. It was M.

"Now what could M mean?" thought Kay. "This is certainly an interesting list."

Instantly she decided not to give up the paper until she could study it carefully. As the cab stopped in front of her house, she slipped the yellow sheet into her pocketbook and paid the driver.

Inside the house, Kay was surprised to find that her mother wasn't home. Clara, the cleaning lady, was there.

"Your mother went away to visit a sick friend," the

woman explained. "She said to tell you she might not get back before late evening. I'm to stay until she comes."

"Did Mother leave me a note, Clara?"

"Yes, it's upstairs in your room."

Kay read the message; then, sprawling flat on the bed, she studied the paper which she had found in the taxicab. Scarcely had she started to scan the list of names when there came a light tap on the door.

"Yes. What is it?"

Clara came in and Kay could see that the woman was disturbed.

"There's someone to see you at the front door."

Kay got up and straightened her dress.

"You should have invited the person into the house. How could you keep anyone waiting outside on a day like this?"

"I wouldn't have done it only he's not very nice," she explained. "A very nasty-looking man. If you take my advice, you won't let him into the house!"

6

An Arrogant Visitor

"Okay, I won't invite him in," promised Kay as she descended the stairs. "I'll just find out—"

She stopped suddenly and gasped. Seated on the sofa, calmly smoking a cigarette, was the man Clara had refused to let in!

As Kay went slowly down the stairs, he stood up and looked at her with a smirk which evidently was intended to be friendly. When Kay didn't speak he said, "You are Mees Kay Drazy?"

Then he walked forward, offering his hand. Kay pretended not to notice the gesture.

"Yes, I am Miss Tracey," she answered, hiding her irritation.

"You and me will do some beezness together, yes?" he announced.

Seating himself again, he blew a smoke ring toward the ceiling.

"I don't know what business we would have together," replied Kay coldly. "You haven't even told me your name."

"Ho! Ho! What eez een a name? That poet, he say: 'A rhoze he smell good if you call heem a cockle-da-burr!"

Kay ignored the man's crude attempt to avoid telling his name. He was dirty and his clothes were a mess and her only thought was to get him out of the house as quickly as she could!

"You have never seen me before," he went on. "But

never mind. I have seen you, Mees Drazy. On the day you have the beeg trouble I see you."

Kay figured that the man was referring to the car accident, though she didn't know how he could have found out about it. She had told no one except for her mother and the Worth twins of Mr Craken's claim for damages.

"I see you on the day of the beeg accident," went on the man. "You need someone to testify you were not in the smash-up, maybe?"

"And you are willing to testify on my behalf?" Kay asked in surprise.

"Sure, I make a nize air-tight alibi for you. Of course you pay me, say a hundred dollars?"

Kay suspected now that she was dealing with a con-man. Still, there was a faint chance that the man might have seen her on the day of the accident. She didn't want to lose track of him until she was certain that he could be of no help to her. At least it would be worth while to find out how the man had heard about the accident.

"I'll have to talk about this with my mother," she said. "A hundred dollars is a lot of money for a witness."

"You be glad to pay eet, I theenk," answered the man as he stood up.

"Where can I get in touch with you?"

"Oh, I come back in a few days," he replied as he walked to the door. "Good-bye, Mees Drazy."

Kay stood at the window and watched the man until he had disappeared around the corner. She distrusted him, yet she thought she might be prejudiced because of his bad manners and unpleasant way of speaking. He really could have seen her on the day of the accident. She had taken a long walk with the dog during the time that the auto smash-up had occurred.

Late that evening when her mother returned, Kay told her about the man's visit. Mrs Tracey agreed that the man would not make a reliable witness, but she said that Kay had been smart to tell him to come back again.

"If only Bill were here," she sighed. "I can't understand why he doesn't come home or at least let us know where he is. If he doesn't come tomorrow I'll be very worried about him as well as you."

"Oh, Bill can take care of himself," responded Kay comfortingly. "I bet he went off somewhere on a secret mission."

"Why do you think that?"

"Well, now that I look back I remember he had hinted for weeks that he might be called away on a mysterious case."

The next day Kay went to the Carmont and Brantwood police stations. She couldn't find any record of the accident, nor was she able to find the policeman who had identified her as the driver of the car which had caused the smash-up. But the police did promise her that a thorough investigation would be made.

Somewhat reassured, Kay decided to drive to Ottenville to find out something about the law firm of Duster and Trout. When she returned home for her car she met Ronald Earle. Kay told him her plans and he said he would take her to the distant town.

"Oh, that would be great!" accepted Kay eagerly. "I'd much rather not make the long ride alone."

She called her mother; then in Ronald's car set out for Ottenville. Driving along Sunset Drive, they soon passed the Huntley mansion. Kay noticed that the blinds were drawn. A car was coming slowly down the driveway.

"That looks like the Eaton car," she observed, turning her head to glance back. "Yes, it's Chris—alone."

"I wonder what she's doing at the Huntley place?" remarked Ronald curiously.

"I can guess. She's probably taking dancing lessons from Monsieur Le Blanc without her mother's knowledge."

When they finally reached the city, Kay realized she had neglected to bring the address of the Ottenville law firm with her. Ronald went to look up the name in a directory. As Kay waited in the car, she suddenly noticed a man crossing the street quickly.

"Why, it's Mr Craken!" she realized. "He must live in Ottenville."

She saw him enter a store and make his way toward a telephone booth. Scarcely had the man disappeared when a sloppily dressed man who had been standing nearby walked slowly past the shop. He looked through the window, then entered the store.

"Mr Craken is being watched!" thought Kay, "and it's that same man who offered to be a witness for me!"

Her curiosity aroused, Kay ran across the street. After a moment's hesitation she went into the store. There was the man standing by the telephone booth, pretending to look at some magazines. Actually he was eavesdropping upon Mr Craken's phone conversation.

The owner of the store, occupied with a customer, did not notice Kay; neither had either of the men she was watching. Quickly she crouched behind one of the high counters. She was now out of sight of both men, yet she could hear the telephone conversation, for Mr Craken spoke in a loud voice.

"Sure, everything's sewed up tight on that Tracey case," she heard him say. "Yeah, the girl's got to be guilty. Nothing to it."

Kay hoped that Mr Craken would reveal more, but he abruptly hung up the phone and hurried from the store. The man who had been eavesdropping waited a moment, then followed.

"He was listening, all right," Kay told herself thoughtfully. "Now I wonder if he really may know something which would help me."

She straightened up from her cramped position behind the counter. Before she could leave the store the owner came to attend her, so she bought a can of soup. Ronald was waiting for her when she returned to the car.

"I bought you a little present," she laughed, dropping the can into his lap. "I thought you might be hungry."

"Say, what is this, a joke?" demanded Ronald.

Kay quickly explained why she had bought it.

"I saw those same two guys come out of the store only a minute ago!"

"Which way did they go, Ronald?"

"The first man started down Cannon Street, and the other followed him."

"Let's follow them! I want to see where Mr Craken goes."

Ronald turned the car around and they drove down Cannon Street to its very end. There was no sign of either Mr Craken or the other man.

"Well, it's no use," Kay decided at last. "Probably they turned on to a side street. Did you get the address of the Duster and Trout firm?"

"It wasn't in the telephone book."

"Then it must be a new firm."

"I asked the druggist. He said he'd never heard of them. Then I stopped two people on the street and they'd never heard of Duster and Trout either."

"Oh, it was so dumb of me to come without the letter," Kay said with annoyance. "At least we found out where Mr Craken lives and that that man has been following him."

"We can drive over again tomorrow," Ronald suggested eagerly. "I'll be glad to bring you."

"Maybe that won't be necessary. If Bill gets home I'll ask him to take care of the whole thing."

Ronald and Kay decided to stop somewhere for ice cream. At the Pickworth Inn the time passed pleasantly and swiftly. It was very late before they finally started toward Brantwood.

"I wanted to stop for a moment at the Huntley house," she remarked as she and Ronald approached the old mansion. "I guess it's too late now."

"You're pretty interested in that place, aren't you?" he teased, glancing at his watch.

"Oh, not in the house. Only in the people who live there. I wish I knew how the Le Blancs happened to rent the place."

"Maybe I could find out for you."

"Oh, Ronald, I wish you could! I think that my double, Jane Barton, has something to do with them."

"Let's stop there now if you think you could pick up any useful information," said Ronald, switching on the car headlights. "It's nearly seven thirty, so we've already missed our dinners."

"How did it get to be so late?" gasped Kay in dismay. "Well, I'll only take a minute. I'll just knock on the door and ask if Jane Barton lives there."

Ronald parked his car in front of the old mansion. A few lights were on upstairs but the lower part of the house appeared to be dark.

"Should I go with you?" Ronald offered, opening the car door.

"It's not necessary. I'll be back in a minute."

Kay ran up the path to the house. Then she hesitated, deciding to try the back door instead of the front. As she rounded the corner and glanced toward the sunken garden, she saw a sight which caused her to stop suddenly.

A ghostly figure could be seen moving around the garden. As Kay watched, it danced gracefully through the ruins and then disappeared into the darkness.

7

The Ghost in the Garden

Kay rubbed her eyes. Was it her imagination, or had she actually seen a dancing ghost in the sunken garden?

To satisfy herself, she went quickly down the stone steps leading to the gazebo. As she got closer she caught another glimpse of the ghost. This time she knew that her eyes had not deceived her. Standing perfectly still, she watched the graceful movements.

"It is someone dancing," she whispered to herself. "And she's really good. I wonder if it could be Jane?"

Kay decided to get closer. In her eagerness she did not notice where she was walking and suddenly she tripped. Her shoe made a loud, grating sound on the cement.

Instantly the white-robed figure stopped dancing. Kay thought she heard a gasp and then the ghost turned and fled deeper into the garden.

"Jane! Jane!" Kay called softly. "Please don't run away. I'm your friend."

There was no answer, only a rustling movement of the bushes. Kay waited a moment, then walked slowly towards the gazebo. It was too dark to see anyone in the garden, yet she sensed that the dancer was lingering somewhere near. She could almost feel a presence. Maybe if she stayed very quiet for a little while the ghost might return.

As Kay sat down on a bench inside the gazebo, she touched something on the seat. She realized it was a picnic basket.

"This isn't the same one that was here the other day," she thought, feeling the handle. "Wait! What's this?"

There was a note tied to the basket handle! Someone had left the empty basket and a message for whoever was supposed to come and get it!

"I'll bet this note will help me figure out this mystery," Kay thought. "I wish I had a flashlight so I could read it here."

Stealthily someone was approaching the gazebo, but Kay didn't hear the steps. Suddenly the bench she was sitting on was knocked over and Kay was tumbled awkwardly to the floor. Quickly she scrambled to her feet and groped about for the lunch basket. It was gone, and so was the note!

To the right, on a path which led towards the river, Kay could hear someone running. She started to follow but soon realized she would never catch up with the person. She was unfamiliar with the trails which wound through the garden, while the person ahead seemed to know every inch of the grounds.

Suddenly Kay stumbled over a trailing rose vine and fell on the stone path. It was a hard fall, and Kay lay still for a minute. Then, hearing her name called, she pulled herself to a sitting position.

"Kay! Kay! Where are you?" It was Ronald's voice.

"Here!" she answered weakly. "Down in the garden."

She kept calling until he found her in the darkness.

"What are you doing here?" he asked, helping her to her feet. "Are you hurt?"

"I twisted my ankle a little and bruised my elbow."

"What happened?"

"I was chasing a ghost and tripped over a rose vine."

"A ghost? Kay, be serious."

"It was a figure dressed in a white robe. Just as I reached the house I saw someone dancing in the garden. When I called to her she ran away."

"Do you think you can walk to the car?"

"Of course," Kay insisted, although her face twisted with

pain as she took a step. She was glad that Ronald could not see the grimace.

"Lean on me all you can," he suggested, helping her up the steps.

Just as they reached the last one a dog began to bark. The animal came bounding toward them from the direction of the house, growling so savagely that Ronald seized a stick.

"Uh-oh, everyone in the mansion will find out that we've been prowling around here," Kay whispered anxiously.

As she spoke the back door of the house opened. Madame Le Blanc's thin figure was silhouetted.

"Who is there?" she called shrilly.

Kay and Ronald stood motionless and didn't answer. To their relief, the dog turned and ran back to his mistress. Taking him by the collar the woman led him into the house.

"I was sure she would see us," Kay laughed nervously when the door had closed. "That was a narrow escape."

When they reached the car, Ronald helped her into the seat.

"I'll take you to a doctor," he said. "I'm worried about your ankle."

"Oh, it's nothing," Kay insisted. "Just a little sprain. Tomorrow I'll be dancing on it. If I went to a doctor he would tell me to keep off it for a day, and I can't do that. Not while we're practising for the benefit show."

The next morning her ankle did feel much better, but Miss Grover thought she shouldn't strain the muscles by dancing. At her suggestion Kay sat and watched the other girls rehearse instead of dancing.

"You're not missing much," remarked Chris Eaton who had come to the gym to watch the rehearsal. "In all my life I never saw such awkward work."

"Well, of course you have the advantage of professional instruction," Kay said mischievously.

Chris gave her a quick, suspicious glance. "What do you mean, Kay Tracey?"

"Aren't you taking lessons from the great dancing master, Monsieur Le Blanc?"

"I didn't say I was, did I?" Suddenly Chris looked frightened. She ran from the gym.

When Kay got home that afternoon her mother still had not heard from Bill. She was very worried.

"I've decided to talk with Bill's secretary," she told Kay. "She's waiting for me at his office. Would you mind doing me a favour while I'm out?"

"Sure, Mother. What is it?"

"Do you remember old Mrs Cary? She has been a semi-invalid for many years now."

"Doesn't she live in a little white cottage beyond Hillman's farm?"

"Yes, not far from the edge of town. Mrs Cary did some sewing for me, and I have neglected to pay her. I wish you would give her this money and tell her I appreciated the work."

Kay put the money in her pocketbook. After her mother had driven away in the car, she called Jerry to come walk with her. After a while she turned into the woods for a short cut.

Kay had not gone very far when she thought she heard footsteps behind her. She didn't see anyone when she looked back, but several times Jerry stopped and growled.

"Someone is following me!" Kay decided nervously.

She quickened her step, taking care to stay near the dog. After a while the footsteps stopped. Kay relaxed, deciding that the person she had heard might have been a hunter. Or perhaps the sound had been made by an animal.

Suddenly Jerry stopped short in the path, pointed his ears, and growled. Before Kay could react a man in shabby clothes darted from behind a pile of brush where he had been hiding. Grabbing her pocketbook, he turned and fled.

8

Mrs Cary's Story

"After him, Jerry!" cried Kay, pointing towards the man.

The dog hadn't waited for an order from Kay; he already had taken up the chase. Catching up with the purse snatcher, he seized his trouser leg and held on until Kay ran over to him.

"Give me my pocketbook!" she yelled angrily.

The man didn't resist as she jerked it from his hand. She saw then that he was not more than twenty years old, and didn't have a vicious-looking face.

"I—I'm sorry," he muttered, hanging his head.

"You followed me from the edge of town," accused Kay.

"I—I was desperate," he said softly. "You don't know—what it means—to be hungry."

Kay couldn't help but feel a little sorry for the young man. She hesitated, then commanded Jerry to release him.

"What's your name," she asked, watching him closely.

"Everyone calls me Joe," he answered. "Joe Kemp. I don't know my real name. My parents left me on a doorstep when I was a baby."

"I guess you've had a hard life," said Kay sympathetically.

"It wasn't so bad until just lately. Now I can't get work and I ran out of money."

"What kind of work have you been doing?"

"Oh, just about everything. My last job was as a machinist. I'd take anything I could get."

"Maybe I can help you," said Kay slowly.

"After the way I tried to steal your pocketbook?"

"I'll forget about that, Joe, if you'll promise to go straight. I'll see if I can find a job for you."

"That would be great!" the young man exclaimed.

"Then you'll give me your promise?"

"I'll never steal again as long as I live. I wouldn't have snatched your purse only I was desperate."

Kay took a few dollars from her pocketbook and gave it to Joe. She also wrote her name and address on a piece of paper for him.

"Here, use this money to buy yourself some food," she instructed. "Then come to my house and I'll see what I can do for you."

As Kay continued on through the woods, she wondered if she had done a foolish thing. Most people would have turned the young man over to the police and forgotten the incident.

"He may never come to the house," she thought. "But if he does, how will I find him a job?"

At Mrs Cary's cottage, Kay temporarily dismissed the problem from her mind. Finally she decided to tell the old lady what had happened to her in the woods.

"Mercy me, I hope that young scamp doesn't hide out in the woods," responded Mrs Cary, rocking nervously back and forth in her chair. "He might try to break into my cottage tonight."

"I don't think he will bother you," Kay said reassuringly. "He didn't seem like a mean person."

"Maybe he just has a weak character," the old lady said. "You can't tell how a young person will turn out these days. Sometimes the ones who have all the advantages end up the worst. Now take that Huntley girl for example—she had as good a chance in life as any person in this town. But what happened to her?"

"What *did* happen?" Kay asked curiously. "I never heard the story, Mrs Cary."

"Huntley wasn't her real name," the old lady explained. "She was a sister to Mrs Huntley, but the two of them were often spoken of as the Huntley girls."

"What was her name?" asked Kay.

"Trixie Rue. She was a dancer and folks said she had a promising career ahead of her. But she married and had a baby. Things didn't go well with her after that. Her husband couldn't make a living. They kept going down and down until finally the poor girl resorted to theft."

"Why didn't the Huntleys help her?"

"Mrs Huntley did try. I know, because I worked for her as housekeeper at the time. Secretly, she would send me to the house with money for Trixie. I guess it wasn't enough to save the girl from disaster."

"Who did Trixie steal from?" Kay asked as the old lady lapsed into silence.

"I can't tell you that. In fact, I'm not sure whether she took the money or whether it was her husband. I gave up my job as housekeeper for Mrs Huntley when she and her husband went to Europe. As I remember, it was about that time Trixie had all her trouble."

"I see," commented Kay thoughtfully. "What finally happened to Trixie and her child?"

Mrs Cary shook her head. "I don't know. They disappeared from Brantwood and weren't heard from again. I never even saw the little girl, because she was in boarding school at the time. Mrs Huntley paid for that, I believe. Oh, it was a sad thing."

"The Huntleys never came back?"

"No. I suppose the disgrace kept them from coming home. Mr Huntley died in Europe soon after they went there. His wife stayed in Paris, and I was told that she passed away too."

Kay was fascinated by the story though she felt disappointed that Mrs Cary didn't know any details of the theft. Her curiosity in the Huntley house had been aroused first by Ronald's hint that a mystery was connected with the place. Kay would love to be able to put all the clues together!

On the way home, Kay realized that with a lawsuit pending against her, she had to devote her energy to her own problems, not Trixie Rue's. Finding that her mother had returned from downtown, she asked about her cousin.

"Bill's secretary hasn't heard a word from him," Mrs Tracey reported. "She's beginning to worry about his absence too, but she thinks he is gathering evidence for an important case."

"I wish Bill had given us a hint when he would return," said Kay. "This lawsuit looks more serious every day."

"We could hire another lawyer, if worst comes to worst," replied Mrs Tracey.

"If I can't have Bill, I'll be my own lawyer!" Kay announced with a laugh. "I'm going to drive over to Ottenville and have a talk with the lawyers at Duster and Trout."

Kay was nervous about this, since by this time she suspected that she was dealing with dangerous people who intended to build up a false case against her for some reason. She decided not to worry her mother further by telling her about the conversation she had overheard in the Ottenville store, but it frightened Kay.

It was getting dark by the time Kay reached the office of Duster and Trout at the address given on her letter. There was no elevator in the building. After climbing two flights of stairs, she entered a sloppily furnished reception room. A girl who was just sitting at her desk chewing gum came over to talk to Kay.

"Something?"

"Yes, I'd like to see Mr Duster or Mr Trout, please."

"They've both left for the day," the girl answered, patting her blonde hair to make certain each curl was in place. "Mr Trout went to see a client, and Mr Duster's playing golf."

"Oh, no, I drove all the way from Brantwood. I guess I should have called first."

"Would you like to leave your name?"

"That wouldn't help me, I'm afraid. I wanted to talk with one of the lawyers about a lawsuit which is being brought against me."

"Say, you're not the Tracey girl?"

"Yes, I am," Kay admitted, adding curiously, "Do you know anything about the case?"

"I know about every bit of business that goes through this office," she boasted. "I type up all the briefs and write most of the letters. Yours was the auto accident case."

"Yes, but I'm sure your firm has no evidence against me."

"Well, you just guess again!" The secretary laughed at Kay. "Mr Trout has three witnesses lined up already. They will all testify that you smashed into Mr Craken's car while driving at a high speed. You injured a passenger and left the scene of the accident. That means a criminal as well as a civil suit. Oh, you were pretty dumb, especially since you were driving someone else's car. You'll pay plenty before you get through."

"I don't think so," Kay answered nervously.

"Mr Duster almost never loses a case," the girl went on boastfully.

"I bet all of them are accident cases."

"Just about. Our firm specializes in accident cases. I'd advise you to settle out of court if you can. You'll get off easier that way."

"Thank you," replied Kay drily. "And now, since you have been so kind as to give me advice, I'd like to give you some of my own. Unless you want to lose your job, don't tell your employers how much information you gave me."

"What do you mean?" the girl demanded in alarm. "I didn't tell you anything—"

Smiling, Kay walked out the door and closed it firmly behind her. As she climbed down the steps, her nervousness returned. She had found out some useful information, but now she was sure that she was in trouble. Already Duster and Trout had three witnesses and she didn't have a single person to testify in her behalf.

"Maybe I'd better get in touch with that strange man who came to the house," she thought, "but he's not really the kind of person I need on my side."

While her suspicions had been aroused, Kay had no way of knowing whether or not the lawyers at Duster and Trout were honest. It was possible they believed Mr Craken's story. On the other hand, they might be deliberately building up false evidence against her.

What did Jane Barton have to do with all this? Had the girl been mistaken for her because they looked alike, or was she working for Mr Craken? It suddenly occurred to Kay that her double might have been used to plant evidence against her!

"Bill told me that dishonest law firms sometimes build up false cases, frightening their victims into paying large sums of money," she remembered. "Maybe that's what they're trying to do to me."

Kay was still thinking about this possibility as she walked back to the street where she had left her car. Suddenly she stopped short and a look of panic came over her face.

The car was gone!

9

Double Trouble for Kay

A big truck now stood at the curb in the place where Kay had left her car.

"Could I have made a mistake?" she asked herself, gazing up and down the long row of parked cars. "I remember stopping near this vacant lot."

Slowly she walked along the street, staring at every automobile.

"It's just no use searching any longer," she decided after she had covered several streets. "The car has been stolen. I'd better notify the police."

Kay reported the theft at the police station and was told that she would be notified if the car was located. Now she had to figure out how she could get home. A taxi would be too expensive. She decided to take a train.

At the train station Kay found out that she would have to wait at least two hours. Realizing that her mother would be worried, she decided to call home.

No one answered, so Kay finally called the Worth twins. After listening to a brief account of what had happened, they assured her they would locate her mother and give her the message.

"Ask her to call me back," Kay suggested.

"Where are you going to wait for the train?" asked Wendy.

"I'm going to eat dinner just across the street at the Mad Hatter's Tea Room. I'll be waiting for the call."

The Mad Hatter's Tea Room turned out to be a pleasant,

inexpensive restaurant and Kay stopped to talk to the cashier.

"Could you let me know if a phone call comes for Kay Tracey?" she requested.

"Yes, certainly."

Kay found a table in a secluded corner of the room. After giving her order to a waitress, she tried again to piece together the mystery.

Kay was so absorbed in her thoughts that she didn't notice a good-looking young man enter the restaurant. He saw her at once. Smiling with delight he came over to her table.

"Hello, there," he said, sliding into the vacant chair opposite her. "I didn't expect to find you in Ottenville."

Kay glanced up and realized that he was the same young man who had spoken to her in the flower shop!

"He has mistaken me for my double again." She thought quickly. "If I pretend I'm Jane Barton, I might be able to find some clues."

"Where have you been keeping yourself lately?" he asked, smiling at her. "Not trying to avoid me, are you?"

"Oh, no," murmured Kay in a slightly nasal voice. She raised her handkerchief so that it half covered her face. "I've been sick. I'm just getting over a bad cold."

"That's too bad," he replied sympathetically. "I noticed that your voice was husky. You look thinner, too."

Kay nodded and hid a smile. It was working! But she must be on her guard constantly or he would realize she was deceiving him.

"I'll bet old Blancky has been working you too hard," the young man went on. "You ought to let me tell him a thing or two!"

"Would that do any good, do you think?"

"It would do *me* a lot of good anyway," he said angrily. "He's a slave driver."

"I have been working hard," Kay answered, taking care to keep her face lowered.

"Sure, Blancky doesn't care about anyone but himself."

Kay wondered if the young man was talking about Monsieur Le Blanc.

"I wish you would give up your career," the young man went on, leaning closer. "You know you can marry me any time you want."

Kay was suddenly grateful that the room was lit only by candlelight. Behind her handkerchief, her face flushed a deep pink. She wished now that she had told the man who she was immediately. The situation was getting complicated.

The telephone rang.

Hearing the sound, Kay jumped and stood up. She was certain that the call was for her.

"You really are nervous!" observed the young man, watching her curiously. "You've definitely been working too hard. You're not yourself at all."

"I certainly am not myself today," Kay agreed, staring at the waitress who was answering the telephone.

Kay saw that the woman was writing down a reservation and she relaxed. The phone call had not been for her. She would be safe for a few minutes longer at least.

Now that it was too late to do anything about it, she realized that she shouldn't have given the cashier her name. If the call should come through she would be identified immediately!

"Maybe I can get him to leave before he realizes I'm not Jane Barton," Kay thought.

A waitress came with Kay's food, and the young man gave her his order.

"I don't think you'll like this place," Kay said discouragingly as she tasted her salad. "If I were you I would cancel my order and try another restaurant."

"Oh, I like the food here," he answered. "I often eat here. Anyway, I don't care what I eat as long as I'm with you."

Kay blushed again and glanced quickly toward the next table. The young man's voice had carried to nearby diners who were listening to the conversation with interest.

"I simply have to talk with you," he went on in a more demanding voice. "When will you give me my answer?"

"Oh—I—don't know," Kay stammered, avoiding his direct glance. "I wish you wouldn't—"

The telephone rang again. This time she was sure it was for her.

"Excuse me," she said quickly. She stood up and went to the telephone. To her annoyance the persistent young man followed her.

"Don't leave now," he protested.

Kay turned away from him but the waitress was already at the phone. She realized that unless she could get rid of him quickly, she would be exposed.

Turning toward him she whispered urgently, "If you go now, I promise I'll meet you here again in a few days."

"When will you meet me?" he asked eagerly.

"In four days."

"Next Tuesday evening?"

"Yes, at eight o'clock," Kay agreed desperately. "Now please go."

She actually gave the young man a little push which started him towards the door, but he was so thrilled by her promise that he scarcely noticed it. He didn't realize how eager Kay was to get him out of the restaurant. Other diners had watched the little scene and were laughing at them.

Kay breathed a sigh of relief, thinking that she was safe. But before the man was out of the door, the waitress called in a loud voice which could be heard plainly throughout the room, "Telephone call for you, Miss Tracey!"

10

Inside the Mansion

Kay glanced towards the door and was relieved to see that the young man hadn't heard her name spoken. "I'll take the call," she said, turning to the waitress.

She was fully aware of the amused glances which were directed toward her as she picked up the phone, but she didn't mind. The other people in the restaurant probably thought that she had sent the young man away so she could make a date with someone else!

The call was from Kay's mother. Wendy and Betty had located her at a neighbour's home and had told her about the theft of the car.

"Now don't worry about it, dear," Mrs Tracey said calmly. "Fortunately we are covered by insurance. You plan to come home on the train?"

"Yes, I should get to Brantwood around nine o'clock."

"I'll look up the exact schedule," Mrs Tracey promised, "and meet you at the station."

"Oh, that won't be necessary—" Kay began, but her mother had hung up the phone.

After finishing her dinner, Kay spent a few minutes reading a newspaper, then walked slowly towards the railway station. There was still three quarters of an hour until train time so she walked along past the station for several blocks.

As she approached a corner, her attention was suddenly drawn to a car without lights. Its front tyres had been rammed sharply into the curb.

"That looks like my car!" she thought, starting to run.

She had been wrong twice before, but as she got closer she was almost certain that the car was hers. Even the scratch on the fender was the same.

"This *is* my car!" Kay shouted.

She pulled open the glove compartment on the dash board. Inside was an old golf score, a discarded letter, and a flashlight, articles which instantly identified the automobile as belonging to the Traceys.

"How lucky," Kay thought as she fitted the key into the ignition. "But how did the car get here?"

It didn't seem likely that thieves would have abandoned the car so near the place from which it had been stolen. Probably the truckdriver who had parked in the space where Kay's car had been had wanted to make a delivery. Deliberately he had pushed her automobile out of the way, steering it way down the hill.

"All the trouble that man has caused me!" Kay thought angrily. "I just wish I had caught him in the act. I must report this to the police."

Upon her earlier visit to the police station, Kay had asked about the Craken accident case, and had been told that nothing had been turned in. The police officer in charge had promised to make an investigation. Now, before leaving the station, she asked if anything new had been learned. The answer was the same as before.

"It's certainly strange," Kay thought as she drove home. "Here I have been sued for damages, yet I can't find a police report against me. It begins to look more and more like a frame-up."

Since her visit to the offices of Duster and Trout she realized how important it was to locate her double. Convinced that Jane Barton lived with the Le Blancs, she thought about whether or not it would be worth while to make one more attempt to contact her there. As Kay drove by the old Huntley mansion, she could see a dim light in the lower windows. She stopped and thought for a moment, and then turned into the driveway. Parking out of sight near the road, she walked up to the house.

Twice she rang the doorbell, but no one answered. Deciding to try the back door, Kay made her way quietly around the house. It was so dark, she could not see a foot in front of her.

Suddenly she heard voices. Two people, a man and a woman, were somewhere in the sunken garden. They were speaking rapidly in French. From the loud tones Kay felt sure they were arguing. At first she could understand nothing, but presently as the man's anger faded, he spoke in English.

"There iss no peaze for me here, *jamais*! Always the quarrel, the bicker, noise, noise, noise! All I ask iss that I be left alone with my art."

"Your art!" exclaimed the woman. "All I hear is talk about your art! Who has made your art schemes possible? My brother!"

"*Oui*, but not with ze honest money."

"I won't allow you to speak like that against Lazarre!" the woman cried angrily. "You are—what you call it—an ingrate!"

By this time Kay had no doubt but that she was listening to a bitter quarrel between Madame Le Blanc and her talented husband. The reference to "dishonest money" fascinated her and she wanted to find out more. As the voices dropped lower, she leaned forward so she wouldn't miss a single word.

Gradually Kay could make out the shadowy forms of the couple, who stood near the ruined pagoda. Their faces were towards her. At the same moment that she definitely identified them as Monsieur and Madame Le Blanc, the latter noticed a movement in the dark.

"Who is there?" she called sharply.

Kay remained perfectly still but couldn't fool the woman.

"I see you *la-haut!*" the woman cried. "On the steps! Who is it?"

Kay didn't answer. Instead she ran up the stone staircase. Then, dodging from bush to bush, she started towards the driveway.

"After her!" screamed Madame Le Blanc to her husband. "We must not let her escape. No!"

Kay was amazed at the speed with which the thin Frenchman could run. Almost before she was aware that he had taken up the chase, she felt his strong hands grasp her arm. In vain she struggled to free herself.

"Non, my *fille*," the dancing master said, giving her a hard little shake. "How many times have I to tell you? Stay out of ze garden!"

Madame Le Blanc came running up. As soon as she had caught her breath, she scolded the girl angrily in French. Kay did not understand much of this, but she kept her head bent low as if she were ashamed of her actions.

"Back into the house!" the woman commanded at the end of her tirade. "Go to your room and to bed!"

Taking Kay firmly by an arm she pulled the girl towards the house. Kay didn't resist because she knew that she had been mistaken for her double. If she played her part well she might get away with it and at the same time gather valuable information!

Madame Le Blanc opened the back door and gave Kay a little push into the kitchen. "Do not come out again, tonight," she ordered sternly. "Go to bed. *Vite!* You understand?"

"*Oui,*" mumbled Kay, keeping her head bent low.

As the door slammed shut behind her, she took a deep breath. She actually was inside the old mansion and free to investigate!

Kay glanced about the kitchen curiously. The sink was piled high with unwashed dishes, but otherwise everything appeared to be in order. Whatever other faults she might possess, Madame Le Blanc was not a messy housekeeper.

A dim light was on in the living room. After making certain that one was there, Kay tiptoed in and looked about. She was disappointed, for the old-fashioned furniture set neatly against the walls was not at all what she had expected.

"Just what did I think I would find here?" Kay asked herself with a smile. "I suppose the house ought to be filled with dancers!"

Moving to the foot of the circular stairway, she listened. The floor above was silent. Either the place was deserted or else the members of the household were asleep. Kay crept quietly up the stairs.

The upstairs hall was dark but she dared not turn on the electric lights. Groping her way along, she came to a closed door.

Kay pressed her ear against the panel and listened. Absolute quiet. It seemed as though the upstairs floor was deserted.

Carefully she turned the knob and pushed open the door a tiny crack. Was it imagination or HAD she heard soft breathing?

After waiting a moment Kay tiptoed through the doorway. The room was absolutely dark. Kay hesitated in the doorway sensing that someone was there.

"Imagination," she told herself sternly.

She started to move forward. Without warning, something gripped her skirt and she was jerked backwards against the door.

11

A Benefit Show

Not realizing that Kay had the car back and was driving to Brantwood, Mrs Tracey and the Worth twins took a cab to the railway station to meet her. As the passengers got off the train, they watched eagerly for a glimpse of her.

"All aboard!" shouted the conductor.

"Oh, the train is pulling out," cried Wendy, glancing about frantically. "Where is Kay?"

"We must have missed her somehow," replied Betty.

"I saw every person who left the car," said Mrs Tracey anxiously. "I don't think she was on the train. That's very strange."

"It isn't like Kay to miss a train," said Wendy as the three walked back slowly to the waiting cab. "Don't worry, Mrs Tracey, I'm sure we'll find her at home when we get there."

When they got back to the Tracey home, only one light was burning in the living room and the front door hadn't been unlocked.

"She hasn't been here!" Mrs Tracey exclaimed even before they entered the house. "Oh, I was afraid of it."

"I guess she must have missed her train," Wendy admitted reluctantly. "When does the next one come?"

"There isn't another until morning. That's why I'm so worried."

"Something unusual must have happened," Betty said slowly. "But it's strange that Kay doesn't call and explain."

"She may be in serious trouble."

"Oh, Kay knows how to look after herself in almost any

situtation," said Wendy comfortingly. "We'll hear from her soon."

The three sat down in the living room to wait. "If only I knew where to reach her I would telephone," Mrs Tracey said nervously. "If she doesn't come soon—"

"A car is turning into the driveway!" cried Wendy, who was sitting near the window.

"A taxicab?" asked Mrs Tracey eagerly.

"I don't think so."

"Then it couldn't be Kay because her car was stolen."

"But it *is* Kay and she has her own car!" exclaimed Wendy, rushing to the door.

Mrs Tracey and Betty followed as fast as they could, surrounding the car before Kay could drive it into the garage.

"Oh, I'm so glad you're home safe," Mrs Tracey declared in relief. "But you said the car had been stolen."

"We worried a lot when you didn't come on the train," added Betty, half accusingly.

"I'm sorry about everything," replied Kay as she got out of the car. "Let me catch my breath and I'll try to explain."

In the living room she told them what had happened to the car and how she had found it just before she went to the train station.

"But why did it take you so long to get here?" asked Betty, who figured that Kay was keeping something back. "You didn't have a flat tyre on the way?"

"No."

"Then what did happen?"

Kay laughed mysteriously. "Oh, not much of anything."

Betty looked at her friend sceptically but decided to let it go for now. However, she made up her mind that when they were alone she would convince Kay to tell her what happened.

"It's so late, why don't you girls stay overnight with

Kay?" invited Mrs Tracey. "If you want to, I'll call your mother."

The twins decided to stay, and no sooner were the three girls in Kay's room than Wendy and Betty both began talking, demanding that she tell everything.

"What do you mean, 'everything'?" asked Kay, searching the bureau for two extra pair of pyjamas.

"Oh, don't pretend," Betty answered. "We know you're keeping something from us."

"What would you say if I told you someone just asked me to marry him?"

Betty sank back on the bed, staring incredulously at her friend.

"You're kidding Kay!"

"No, I'm not. A very handsome man, too, a few years older than me, with beautiful brown eyes. He says I must give up my career."

"Your career!" gasped Wendy. "*What* career?"

"I'm not sure." Kay confessed with a laugh.

"Are you teasing us?" demanded Betty suspiciously.

"How can you suggest such a thing?" asked Kay. "He proposed to me at the Mad Hatter's Tea Room in Ottenville."

"Kay, you must have been dreaming," Betty accused. "You can't expect us to believe all this really happened, unless—hey, were you mistaken for your double again?"

Kay nodded and laughed. "Yes, that's what happened. I had a very exciting time being my unknown twin!"

Wendy and Betty both began asking questions at the same time, and finally Kay told them everything that had happened at the restaurant.

"And you promised to meet him again?" Wendy asked.

"Yes, I had to get rid of him quickly and that was the only way I could think of. Anyway, it occurred to me that by talking with him again I might be able to find out something about this double of mine."

"Maybe he was only leading *you* on," suggested Betty. "I'd be careful if I were you, Kay."

"Oh, I will. If only I could find out his name before next Tuesday!"

"What will you say when he asks you to marry him again?" Wendy asked.

"I'll have to think about that. When the time comes I'll get out of the situation somehow."

Wendy shook her head. She thought Kay was walking straight into trouble.

"Have you heard anything from Bill?" Betty inquired after a moment.

"Not a word," Kay answered. "I really am getting worried about him."

"I think you're making a mistake not to go to the police," said Wendy. "Maybe he was kidnapped!"

"Oh, Wendy, you always think of the worst possibilities," protested Betty. "I can't believe anything like that has happened."

"Neither can I," added Kay as she quickly changed the subject. "Do you want to hear a good joke on me?"

"Yes," said Betty.

"It happened at the Huntley mansion. I stopped there again, and I overheard an argument between Monsieur Le Blanc and his wife. To make a long story short, they caught me. Thinking that I was Jane Barton, they sent me into the house."

"So that was why you were so late in getting home!" interrupted Betty. "Then what happened?"

"I decided to do a little exploring. The house seemed deserted, but I thought Jane Barton might be sleeping upstairs."

"I thought this was supposed to be a joke," said Wendy. "It sounds serious to me."

"I didn't get to the funny part yet. Well, as I was saying, I stole up the stairway and opened one of the bedroom doors. I thought I heard someone breathing softly but I couldn't be sure. Then suddenly, as I moved forward, my skirt was grabbed!"

"Oh, Kay!" Betty shuddered. "Weren't you frightened half to death?"

"How did you get away?" asked Wendy tensely.

"Oh, it wasn't very difficult. I just unhooked the pocket of my dress from the door knob!"

"You mean—it wasn't anyone?" demanded Betty. "You had just caught your dress?"

"That was all, but I'll admit I was as scared as if someone actually had grabbed me! Right away I decided to postpone further investigation. I figured that Mother would be worrying about me, and anyway, I was glad to get out of the house before I was caught."

"Then you didn't find out whether anyone besides Monsieur Le Blanc and his wife live in the house?" inquired Betty curiously.

"No, I didn't. Do you think I should have gone on?"

"I don't even think you should have gone as far as you did," Wendy replied. "Be glad you escaped and don't go back"

"We'll see," laughed Kay as she jumped into bed.

The next day, the three girls had just got to school when they were met by one of the members of the dance club.

"Hi," Kay greeted her. "Have you sold any tickets yet for the Children's Home benefit?"

"No," the girl answered, "and I don't think I will. I doubt if anyone will sell any tickets."

"What do you mean?" Kay asked in astonishment.

"You haven't heard about Chris Eaton's show?"

"Chris is giving a show?"

"She isn't taking part in it herself, but she's selling tickets. It's the same night as our benefit."

"That shouldn't keep many people away from our show."

"Chris has sold a lot of tickets already," the other girl said. "It's a movie at the Rialto with some dance numbers as a special attraction. She's selling the tickets for half the price of ours and she's telling everyone that it is a much better show!"

"That's downright mean!" said Kay indignantly. "Maybe if we ask her to change the date—"

"She'll never do it, Kay. I think she set it that way on purpose so it would conflict with our affair. She claims the money is to be turned over to a charitable organization."

"I'll talk with her myself," Kay declared. "Since it's a movie it easily could be held some other evening."

The girls found Chris in the locker room. "Chris, you must have known the date we are to appear," Kay protested. "Our advertisements have been up for a week. Why not change your show to a later date so there will be no conflict?"

"Why don't you change yours?" Chris answered impudently.

"You know we can't. The date was set by the committee for the Children's Home benefit. There will be other acts besides ours."

"Well, all arrangements have been made for my show too. You should see the number of tickets I've sold! Seven this morning."

"Please, Chris—"

"I can't change the date even it I wanted to," Chris said as she turned abruptly away. "The manager of the Rialto said he had no other day open."

Kate was thoroughly disgusted at the girl's selfish attitude, but she made up her mind not to give up without a struggle. After school that afternoon she visited the manager of the Rialto Theatre, explaining the situtation to him.

"Arrangements were made for the picture through Mr

Eaton," he told her. "I merely set the date which he requested. It can be changed to the following week."

Relieved, Kay rushed home and called Chris, telling her about the conversation. There was a long moment of silence, then the girl said stiffly, "Sorry, Kay, but it would be out of the question to change the date now. I've sold hundreds of tickets. I never could notify everyone."

"I'll be glad to help you."

"It's just impossible, that's all. And I wish you wouldn't keep bothering me about it!" Chris hung up the phone before Kay could say more.

At first, members of the dance club didn't think that the movie would offer serious competition, even if the tickets were sold at a lower price than their own. Miss Grover, when told of the situation, refused to be disturbed.

"We must redouble our efforts, that's all," she said cheerfully. "If each girl sells at least twenty, the affair will be a success."

"Twenty tickets shouldn't be hard to get rid of," Betty declared cheerfully. "I know right now where five will go."

"I'll start to work just as soon as I get home from school," announced Kay excitedly.

Her first sale was to her mother. Then she decided to try all her neighbours. At the first house no one was at home. At the next place she was gently but firmly turned down. After stopping at several other places with no better luck, she heard something very upsetting. One woman frankly revealed that she had heard the benefit show would not be very good and she had bought tickets for the movie.

"I'm getting nowhere," Kay told herself as she walked home slowly. "Two hours wasted and only one ticket sold. It begins to look as if Chris has not only sold a lot of tickets, but really put down our performance too! Our show will be a dismal failure."

12

Wanted—A Witness

Kay hoped that other members of the dance club would have better luck, but she called Betty and Wendy and was told they had sold only a few tickets, and those to close friends.

"We're not beaten yet," Kay said grimly. "The battle is just starting. Let's try harder than ever, and not even hint to Chris that we are having a difficult time."

As she hung up the telephone, the doorbell rang. Mrs Tracey answered it. A moment later she came into the living room with a slightly bald-headed man of about forty. He was carrying a briefcase.

"Kay, this is Mr Trout," said her mother. "He wants to talk to you."

"Mr Trout of the firm of Duster and Trout?"

"Yes, quite right," agreed the man, firmly shaking the girl's hand. "I thought you might come to see us, but since you didn't I decided to come to you. You received our letter?"

"Yes, I did," Kay answered as she sat down opposite the lawyer, "and I must say I was very confused. I wasn't in an automobile accident."

The lines about Mr Trout's mouth tightened and his eyes became hard.

"My dear young lady," he said in a patronizing tone. "I realize that your situation is a difficult one, but it will do you no good whatsoever to deny the facts. We have our witnesses. The case is air tight. I therefore advise you, in your own interests, to settle out of court."

"Just what do you suggest, Mr Trout?"

"Mr Craken, our client, is a very nervous man, and I might add a most tolerant one. He doesn't want to become involved in a lawsuit. For this reason he has agreed to accept five thousand dollars to settle the claim."

"Five thousand dollars!" Kay shouted in shock.

"This is ridiculous!" exclaimed Mrs Tracey. "Even if my daughter had been involved in an accident, your client offered to settle for the damages to the car."

"At that time Mr Craken did not realize the extent of injuries to one of his passengers."

"Your client may have a case against someone, but not against me," Kay said calmly. "Apparently another girl was mistaken for me."

"It will get you nowhere to take such an attitude, Miss Tracey. Our case is complete. Will you settle out of court or shall we sue?"

At first Kay had been unable to decide whether or not Mr Trout was an honourable lawyer, but now she realized that he was a hard and ruthless man. His reluctance to listen to any explanation convinced her that he was determined to push his case regardless of the facts.

"You may do as you please," she responded coldly. "I'll not pay you one penny."

"You are prepared to fight the case?"

"Certainly." Kay was bluffing now. "I'll produce witnesses and prove that I wasn't anywhere near the scene of the crash."

"You are making a big mistake."

"I think not," Kay said, gaining confidence. "My cousin is a lawyer and he will take charge of the case for me."

A peculiar expression came over Mr Trout's face but neither Mrs Tracey nor her daughter could figure out what it meant.

"Very well, if that is your decision," he replied, standing

up. "I hope you will change your mind before it is too late."

Nodding to Mrs Tracey, he picked up his briefcase and left the house.

"I don't trust that man at all," Kay's mother declared as soon as he had left the porch.

"I'm sure he is dishonest," the girl agreed. "The idea of demanding five thousand dollars! It makes me furious! I'll fight to the bitter end before I'll give in to blackmail."

"That may not be so easy," said her mother. "You have no witnesses, Kay. Bill isn't here. Everything is in such a mess. We might lose the case. Then in addition to the damages we would have to pay court costs."

"I realize that, Mother. Unless I can find at least one reliable witness, I suppose it would be a waste of money to go into court."

"The women who were here for lunch would say that they saw you here at the house during the early afternoon."

"Yes, but the accident happened while I was out for a walk, or at least that is what they will claim. Oh, if only that strange man who came here the other day could be trusted!"

The following morning, while at a supermarket with the Worth twins, buying fruit and vegetables for her mother, she suddenly caught sight of the man who had come to her home. He was standing, selecting oranges from a box of marked-down fruit. Pointing him out to her friends, Kay said in a whisper, "There is that same fellow who offered to be a witness for me. Don't let on that you see him. I'm going to make up a crazy story, and by telling it to you maybe I can find out how much he really knows about where I was on the day of the accident."

Raising her voice slightly, Kay then began to tell her friends a ridiculous story.

"It's all so silly, their claim that I was in a car crash. On the afternoon of the accident I spent nearly four hours at the zoo. I sat in front of the monkey cage at least an hour. It was just my bad luck that no one saw me there."

She chatted on, fully aware that the man was listening intently. After a few minutes he walked away and Kay stopped talking.

"What do you expect to find out by telling such a silly story?" demanded Betty, deeply puzzled.

"That man listened to every word I said. If he really saw me on the day of the accident, he'll realize it was just a silly story. But if he's only looking for a chance to earn easy money, then I think he'll come to me and claim he saw me at the zoo."

"I hope you're right," said Betty. "But what will you do if he's not a real witness?"

"I just don't know. Jerry will be my only witness, and he can't talk. It's too bad he's only a dog."

Wendy smiled as she recited the first stanza of a poem which came to her mind:

"'I'm a lean dog, a keen dog, a wild dog, and lone; I'm a rough dog, a tough dog, hunting on my own; I'm a bad dog, a mad dog, teasing silly sheep; I love to sit and bay the moon, to keep fat souls from sleep.'"

"Oh, Jerry hasn't any of those vices," Kay laughed as the girls walked home with their baskets. "He's an adorable animal and very smart. Every morning he brings in the paper and he's always amazing me with his new tricks."

At dinner that evening Kay was not at all surprised to receive a call from the strange man. Slumping comfortably into an arm chair, he asked if she had been thinking over his offer to serve as a witness.

"Yes, but I haven't made up my mind yet," she replied evasively. "I'm not entirely convinced that you saw me on the day of the accident."

"Ho! I see you all right, Mees Drazy."

"Where was I?"

"I see you at the zoo. For a long time you stay by the monkey house."

Kay's heart sank, for now she knew that the man had not seen her at all. His only interest in the case was to make money.

"I have decided not to use your testimony," she told him angrily.

The man looked at her as if he could not believe his own ears. He had felt certain she would accept his offer.

"But I hear you say—"

"That's it exactly," interrupted Kay. "You did hear me tell my friends I had been at the zoo, but I was making up the story merely to test you. Now go away and don't annoy me again."

The disappointed man arose. Without a word he left the house, glad that the smart young lady had said nothing about arrest.

Five minutes later the doorbell rang. Kay arose impatiently from the dining room table, thinking that the con-man might have returned to try again. Her expression quickly changed as she recognized Joe.

"Maybe I've come at an awkward time," he apologized self-consciously.

"No, not at all. Come right in."

As Kay led him into the living room, Jerry, who had been lying in front of the fireplace, scrambled to his feet. The dog growled, then made a rush at the man.

"Jerry!" cried Kay, seizing her pet by the collar. "What is the matter with you? Lie down!"

Only after she had repeated the order several times did the dog obey. Even then he eyed Joe with distrust and continued to growl.

"I can't understand it," the girl said in bewilderment. "Jerry was never like this before."

"I guess he remembers how mean I treated you once," Joe said unhappily.

"Have you had your dinner?" Kay asked to change the subject.

"I had a bowl of soup down at the diner."

"Then you must have something more here," she insisted.

Mrs Tracey quickly set another place at the table.

"I suppose you're interested in getting that job I promised you," Kay said as they were finishing dinner.

"I sure could use one."

Kay hadn't really thought about Joe's problem for she had never expected that he would come to the house. However, it suddenly occurred to her that Ronald's father might be able to help.

Excusing herself, she went to the telephone to call Mr Earle. She was very happy when he said he thought he could help.

"Send him around to my office in the morning," he instructed Kay. "I'll find something for him, although I can't say how much it will pay until after I've talked with him."

When Joe heard the good news his voice became husky. Tears came into his eyes as he tried to express his appreciation.

"I'll earn my pay," he promised, taking the address which Kay gave him. "The chance to get back on my feet means a lot to me."

"Mr Earle is a nice man," said Kay, walking to the door with Joe. "I'm sure you'll enjoy working with him."

"I'd enjoy working for anyone after what I've been through."

Jerry arose from the fireplace again, growling low. Joe turned to gaze at the dog.

"Before I was down and out I knew a girl who had a dog almost like yours," he said slowly. "Funny thing too, she looked enough like you to be your sister. Her name was Jane Barton."

13

A Difficult Role

Joe's words excited Kay, but she said very calmly, "I've been told before that I have a double. Does this girl, Jane Barton, really look very much like me?"

"You're as alike as two peas in a pod, but your voices are different."

"I'd like to meet her. Does she live in Brantwood?"

"I don't know where she is now," he admitted. "A year and a half ago she lived with an old lady and her dog at the same furnished apartment house where I stayed. I guess they must have been pretty poor because rents were low there. She really worked hard. She practised dancing all the time. Some of the tenants complained about the noise, but I didn't mind."

"The girl lived with her mother?"

"I never knew if the old lady was a relative or not. The two of them always kept to themselves. Then one day the girl up and disappeared. Next, we didn't see the dog around, and finally the old lady went away."

"You think something happened to them?" Kay asked in amazement.

"Well, I wouldn't say that," Joe replied. "But when I asked the landlady about them, she didn't seem to have any information. A little later I got down on my luck so I pulled out and forgot all about it until I saw you."

Kay asked Joe a few more questions, making a mental note of the apartment house where he had lived.

Immediately after school the following day, Kay and her

mother stopped by the Earle home and were delighted to find out that Joe Kemp had been given a job in Mr Earle's factory. As they were leaving, Ronald pulled Kay aside to tell her something he had found out about the Huntleys.

"Yesterday Mother was talking with old Mr Haynes, who used to look after the family's affairs," he revealed. "It seems that after the Huntleys left here and went abroad they turned all their business over to a foreign lawyer. While they were in France they made new wills."

"Did you find out whom they left the estate to?"

Ronald shook his head. "Mr Haynes never was able to get any information. He told Mother he wrote the lawyer a letter a long while ago, but received no answer."

"It's all very interesting," said Kay.

"Yes, but I'm afraid it doesn't help solve the mystery. By the way, Kay, have you heard anything more from the Ottenville firm?"

"Not since Mr Trout came to see me. I'm driving over to Ottenville tonight."

Kay regretted her words the instant she had spoken, for Ronald immediately replied, "I'm not doing anything special. I'll take you over."

"W-e-l-l," stammered Kay, "Wendy and Betty are going with me. I don't think it would be much fun for you."

"That's okay. But I don't want you to take risks, Kay. You're up to some scheme, and it may be a dangerous one."

"It isn't dangerous at all," Kay laughed.

She wasn't sure what he would think about the meeting with the strange young man, scheduled for that evening at eight o'clock in the Mad Hatter's Tea Room. Kay had been very nervous about this and had even thought about not showing up, but she still had no plan which would solve the mystery.

That evening, on the way to Ottenville with the Worth twins, she explained what she intended to do.

"I'll go to the tea room early, and after I have been there five minutes I want you girls to call me there. Say I'm needed at home. I'll make that reason my excuse for leaving, but I'll say I'll meet him there Saturday."

"You'll go without even seeing your date?" Betty asked in surprise.

"Yes, it's the only safe way," insisted Kay.

"Why bother to drive over to Ottenville at all?" protested Wendy. "If I were you I'd just forget the whole thing."

"I want to keep in touch with this stranger, because through him I may be able to trace Jane Barton. If only I could find out his name!"

"Imagine receiving a proposal of marriage from someone you don't know," said Betty teasingly.

"And picture the poor guy sitting there in the tea room, alone and broken-hearted, waiting for a sweet-heart who never comes," added Wendy mischievously.

"Well, what do you think I should do?" Kay asked with a smile. "Meet him as I agreed and promise to marry him?"

"Your plan is a good one," Wendy replied seriously. "Betty and I will do anything we can to help carry it through."

The girls reached the Mad Hatter's Tea Room at twenty minutes before eight.

"We're later than I thought we would be," Kay said uneasily as she parked the car across the street from the restaurant. "After I go inside don't wait very long before calling me. My date may get here early."

"We'll call in exactly five minutes," promised Betty.

Entering the restaurant, Kay looked to be sure that the young man was not there. As she passed the cashier's desk, the woman remarked with a knowing smile:

"I guess you're looking for that handsome boyfriend of yours. He isn't here yet."

"I'm not supposed to meet him until eight o'clock," replied Kay with a nervous giggle. "When he comes just tell him I'm at the corner table."

Kay sat down and began to read the menu.

"Too bad I won't be able to eat here," she thought with regret. "Everything looks very good."

In a few minutes the telephone rang, and a moment later Kay was told the call was for her. After a fake conversation with Betty, Kay turned to the cashier.

"Something has happened and I must leave right away. If my friend comes will you give him a message? Tell him I wouldn't have left only it's terribly important. I'll meet him here Saturday night."

"I'll tell him, Miss Tracey."

"Oh, one more thing," Kay added with another giggle. "Please don't tell him my name. I'm trying to keep him guessing!"

"That's the way, dearie," laughed the woman. "I'll give him your message."

Kay hastily joined the Worth twins who were waiting beside the car.

"Now where? Home?" inquired Betty as she slid into the front seat.

Kay shook her head. "I have one more favour to ask. I want you girls to go into the restaurant, order some coffee and wait for the strange man to appear. Find out if the cashier gives him my message. Keep your eyes and ears open, and learn anything you can."

"How long shall we stay if the young man doesn't come?" inquired Betty as she and Wendy alighted.

"Oh, until eight thirty, I guess. But I think he'll be there all right."

Kay had not been waiting more than ten minutes when she caught sight of the handsome stranger walking quickly down the street. He didn't look in her direction, but went right into the restaurant. Minutes passed. He did not return.

"Evidently he decided to eat his dinner," Kay thought, glancing at her watch. "Oh, I wish I could go in there myself!"

Another ten minutes passed. Time was going so slowly and Kay was growing restless so she went into a corner store and bought a newspaper. As she came out again, she glanced down the street.

Her heart skipped a beat. Walking swiftly toward her was Mr Craken!

Holding the newspaper in front of her face, Kay ducked into the parked car. The man didn't see her. Crossing the street, he entered the Mad Hatter's Tea Room.

If Kay had been impatient before, she now was totally consumed with curiosity. Had Mr Craken gone into the Mad Hatter's Tea Room to meet the mysterious young man? It was sheer torture not to know what was happening inside.

"Betty and Wendy probably won't pay any attention to Mr Craken because they won't recognize him," she thought miserably. "I wish I could go in there."

A half hour passed, during which time Kay scarcely took her eyes from the building. Then suddenly out came Mr Craken and the strange young man!

14

The Twins Play Sleuth

Kay was tempted to follow the two men, but she didn't want to abandon Wendy and Betty. It was possible too that the twins had important information which she should know. While she was trying to decide what to do, the girls came out of the building and ran to the car.

"Oh, we've learned a lot!" Betty cried excitedly.

"Tell me quickly," Kay urged, her eyes upon the two men who were disappearing down the street.

"We ought to keep that pair in sight," advised Wendy. "Start the car, and we'll tell you everything as we drive."

Kay nodded. Turning the car around, she drove slowly after the two men. Now and then she was forced to pull up at the curb for a moment so that she would not catch up with them.

"We did just what you told us to," said Betty, beginning the story. "We sat down at a table and waited. In a few minutes the man entered."

"Did the cashier give him my message?" asked Kay.

"Yes, she repeated it just as you had told her to do."

"She didn't tell him my name?" Kay asked anxiously.

"No, he seemed to assume that you were Jane Barton, and the woman didn't correct him."

"Then what happened?"

"He went over and sat down at the table opposite ours."

"Wasn't that lucky."

"Yes, it was," agreed Betty, her eyes sparkling. "Well, after a while another man came in and sat down at the same table."

"That was Mr Craken, the one who claims I wrecked his car."

"He called your friend Hal Peterson."

"What did they talk about?"

"We couldn't hear much of the conversation," Betty admitted regretfully. "Mr Craken did advise the young man to pay up or lose his job."

"Pay up what, I wonder?"

"We couldn't figure it out."

"You both did a great job," Kay said excitedly. "I agree that we should follow the two men and learn some more about them if we can."

Before the two men had gone another block they paused at a parking lot.

"Well, we'll talk it over again," Hal Peterson said and climbed into his car, a black sedan, and drove away. Mr Craken walked slowly down the street in the opposite direction.

"Now what are we going to do?" asked Betty. "We can't follow them both!"

Before Kay could answer, the sound of an automobile horn caused the three girls to glance towards the right.

"It's Ronald Earle!" exclaimed Betty in surprise. "I wonder what he's doing in Ottenville?"

"I can guess," Kay muttered under her breath. Then she warned quickly, "Don't you girls dare tell him that I had a date to meet Hal Peterson. I'd have to do too much explaining," she grinned.

Ronald came over to the car.

"So you decided to join our party after all?" Kay asked with a smile.

"I was talking with your mother, Kay. She was afraid you might get into trouble. So I offered to drive over and try to keep you out of mischief," Ronald explained.

"You arrived just in time, too."

Kay didn't think that her mother had been so worried, but she pretended to accept the story. She was really very pleased that Ronald was so concerned about her. Without taking time to provide many details, she told him why they had to follow the two men.

"Will you help us, Ronald?"

"Of course!"

"Then, Betty, you and Wendy take my car and trail Mr Craken. Ronald and I will try to overtake Hal Peterson. We'll have to hurry or we'll lose him."

"Where should we meet?" asked Betty as she exchanged places with her friend.

"In front of the Mad Hatter's. If Ronald and I don't return within a reasonable time, you might as well go home."

The two cars separated. For a few minutes Kay was afraid that they had lost the black sedan but at the second traffic light they came to she caught a glimpse of it. After that Ronald had no difficulty in following. Within a short time they came to the outskirts of Ottenville.

"It looks as if we're starting out for a long ride," Kay worried. "How much petrol do you have, Ronald?"

"Enough to take us at least sixty miles," he replied.

Hal Peterson was a fast driver, but not a reckless one. Seldom did the needle of the speedometer drop below fifty miles an hour as Kay and Ronald trailed the car ahead. They were beginning to wonder how much longer the chase would last when the young man stopped at a country inn.

"Shall we follow him inside the place?" Ronald asked as he parked the car alongside the black sedan.

"I don't dare because he would recognize me right away," Kay answered. "But I have to find out why he came here. Ronald, would you mind—"

"Going in there alone? Not at all, but I don't think I'll make a very good detective. What am I supposed to find out?"

"See if he has a room here or if he came to meet someone. Get any information you can."

Leaving Kay in the car, Ronald entered the inn. Within ten minutes he was back again, looking disturbed.

"No luck?" Kay inquired anxiously.

"Oh, I'm not good at this detective business. I never know the right questions to ask."

"Did you see the man, Ronald?"

"Yes. He was at the desk when I entered, talking with the clerk. I heard him ask if there was any mail for Henry Peterson or a telegram from the Dryden Agency."

"The Dryden Agency," Kay repeated, memorizing the name. "Well, that may be worth knowing."

"The clerk asked him, 'How's business?' and he answered, 'I had a good day.' There's certainly nothing very significant about that. After the fellow went upstairs to his room, I tried to pump the clerk, but I didn't get very far. He told me that Peterson was a 'nice guy' and then switched the subject."

"I hope he didn't suspect why you were questioning him," said Kay anxiously.

"I pretended I was inquiring about rates for an aunt of mine. He seemed to accept the story."

"We've learned everything we can, I guess," Kay remarked after a moment. "Let's drive back to town and meet the twins."

"I'm sorry I didn't do a better job," Ronald repeated. "I never was meant to be a detective."

"You found out some important facts," replied Kay. "The case is progressing slowly but surely. The twins may have something worthwhile to report."

Returning to Ottenville, Kay and Ronald parked in front of the Mad Hatter's Tea Room according to the prearranged plan. After waiting three quarters of an hour for the girls, they decided that it would be useless to remain longer. When they arrived at the Tracey home some time later, they were relieved to find that Wendy and Betty were there ahead of them.

"We just about gave you up," Betty greeted the couple excitedly. "What happened, anyway?"

"We had a little adventure out in the country," explained Kay. "Mr Peterson is staying at an inn about ten miles from Ottenville."

"Wendy and I had an adventure too," reported Betty, lowering her voice. "After we left you, Mr Craken went to his automobile. He drove out of town, stopping at a filling station. While the attendant was putting petrol in the car he went into the office and made a phone call."

"Did you hear the conversation?"

"Yes, we did, at least part of it," Wendy answered triumphantly. "Betty and I walked in, pretending we wanted to buy some candy. He didn't even notice us."

"What did he say, Wendy?" Kay asked eagerly.

"We heard him ask, 'Maggie?' Then he said, 'I'll be right home.' There was a little pause before he added, 'That's not so good, but keep him there.'"

"You're certain he said 'Keep him there?'"

"Oh, yes, Betty and I both heard the words distinctly."

"Did you follow him after he left the filling station?"

"He went to a small town about five miles away—Creston," revealed Betty.

"I was under the impression he lived in Ottenville," said Kay thoughtfully.

"Well, we trailed him to this town. He stopped in the business section and talked for a few minutes with a man he called Lazarre."

"Lazarre!" exclaimed Kay, startled by the information. "Madame Le Blanc mentioned him as her brother!"

"He seemed to be a very nasty man," said Wendy. "We heard him yell at Mr Craken very angrily for not doing some sort of job."

"What else did you find out?"

"That was all," Betty answered regretfully. "It was late and we thought we would miss you and Ronald, so we went back to the tea room. After waiting there about twenty minutes we came to Brantwood."

Kay was excited about the information and thanked the twins for their help. She regretted that they hadn't followed Mr Craken to his home, but now that she knew the town in which he lived she thought it should be fairly easy to find out more about him.

"I have a lot of clues," she thought. "They don't all fit together, but with a little more information I should be able to solve the accident case, and maybe the mystery of the Huntley mansion too.

"Somehow Mr Craken, Lazarre, the Le Blancs, that young man Peterson, and my mysterious double, Jane Barton, are all associated," she reflected. "There must be a key to the situation if only I could find it!"

In the morning Kay awoke with a daring plan worked out in her mind. She would call Hal Peterson and pretend that she was the girl with whom he was in love! If he didn't recognize her voice the plan wouldn't work.

While her mother was busy in the kitchen, Kay made a long distance call to the inn. Soon she heard a sleepy voice say, "Hello? This is Hal Peterson."

Kay's heart was pounding, but she did not lose her courage.

"I hope I didn't get you out of bed," she said. "I thought after failing to meet you last night I owed you an apology. You know who this is, don't you?"

"Mary Jane Rue!" the young man exclaimed. "Oh, I'm so glad to hear your voice. I didn't recognize it at first."

Kay became so excited that for an instant she could think of nothing to say. At last she had definitely established the name of her mysterious double! To Hal Peterson, at least, the girl was known not as Jane Barton, but as Mary Jane Rue!

15

The Deserted Boathouse

Having acquired the information she sought, Kay quickly ended the telephone conversation and ran to the kitchen where her mother was frying eggs.

"Oh, Mother!" she cried excitedly. "I've got a great clue. My double has two names, Jane Barton and Mary Jane Rue. Do you suppose she could be related to that dancer, Trixie Rue?"

"Dear me, how could I guess?" replied Mrs Tracey. "Aren't you jumping at conclusions?"

"Yes, but it's logical, Mother. Oh, this case is really getting to be interesting."

"It won't seem so pleasant if we have to pay five thousand dollars to that man Craken."

"We'll never pay it, I'm sure of that, Mother. The entire case is beginning to take shape."

"I can't make head nor tail of it myself," confessed Mrs Tracey. "You talk about so many people who seem to have no connection with one another."

"But they do, Mother! This is the way I sum it up: Mrs Trixie Rue is Mrs Huntley's sister, and there is a possibility that Jane Rue might be her daughter. Then I know that Lazarre, who made money dishonestly, is Madame Le Blanc's brother."

"You spoke also of an old lady who lived with Jane Barton."

"I'm not sure where she fits into the case," Kay admitted, frowning. "And the dog—"

Her gaze wandered to Jerry, who was curled up by the kitchen stove.

"Mother, I have it!" she exclaimed suddenly. "I know now why he followed me home! It came to me just then in a flash!"

"He?" inquired Mrs Tracey, who was not a mind reader.

"Jerry. Oh, this may turn out to be the best clue yet!"

"What has Jerry to do with the case, Kay? Really, you are talking in absolute riddles."

"Joe told me that my double lived with an old lady and a dog. He said that first the girl disappeared, then the dog. I think Jerry ran off to try to find his mistress!"

"And you believe that he mistook you for her because you look like her?" Mrs Tracey asked.

"No, Jerry would be too smart to make such a mistake. I think he knew the difference, but when he couldn't find her he decided I was enough like her to be a friend."

"It's an interesting theory, Kay." Mrs Tracey gazed doubtfully at Jerry, whose ears were cocked as if he were listening to the conversation. "However, it seems a little far-fetched to me."

"Wait until I find Mary Jane Barton and you'll see," laughed Kay. Then the smile faded from her face. "In a way, Mother, I almost hope you are right, because if I prove my theory I'll lose Jerry!"

Kneeling beside the dog, she hugged him and spoke to him affectionately.

"Strange how he always responds when I call him Jerry," she remarked, half to herself. "Sometimes I wonder if that could be his real name."

At school that day Kay mentioned her theories to Betty and Wendy, telling them she intended to find additional clues.

"I'm going to drive to the old Huntley place as soon as classes are over," she said. "Will you girls come with me?"

"We can't," Betty protested. "Have you forgotten? We're having dance club practice again, and if we get through in time we're supposed to sell tickets."

"Everyone should work especially hard too," added Wendy seriously, "because it looks like the benefit is going to be a complete failure. Chris Eaton is telling everyone that our show isn't worth seeing."

"She really has been mean," agreed Kay angrily. "I'll get rid of my tickets if I have to give them away!"

Kay wanted to help the Children's Home Benefit in every possible way, but she felt she owed herself a certain duty also. The Craken case might be in court soon and she had to produce evidence to prove her innocence. Before deciding what to do she talked over the matter with Miss Grover.

"There is no reason why you can't be excused from rehearsal this afternoon," the teacher assured her. "You know all the dance steps much better than the other girls, and you won't lose anything by missing one practice session."

Relieved, Kay rushed home as soon as school was dismissed.

"Mother, are you very, very busy?" she asked, entering the living room.

"Why no, dear."

"Then I wish you would help me. Our benefit show will be a failure unless we can sell a lot of tickets. I intended to try again today but I have to go out to the Huntley place. Would you mind calling up a few of your friends and suggesting that our cause is a worthy one?"

"I'd rather walk over hot coals than sell tickets," sighed Mrs Tracey as she laid aside her sewing. "But I will do it. It just isn't right for Chris Eaton to deprive those unfortunate children."

"You're great, Mother," Kay said, giving her a hug. "I know you'll be able to sell far more tickets than I could."

Kay called Jerry and they left for the Huntley mansion. Instead of stopping there, she drove nearly half a mile past it to a small village on the river. Parking her car at a boat dock, she sought the man in charge. She had decided to look at the Huntley estate from the water, so she rented a canoe.

"It will be two dollars an hour," he told her, removing a paddle from the rack. "Do you want a canoe or a flat bottom boat?"

"A canoe, please," Kay replied without stopping to think about it. "I have a long distance to paddle, and I'd like to get there quickly."

"The narrow bottom canoes upset easily," the man warned her as he dragged a boat into the water. "I suppose you know how to swim?"

"Oh, yes."

Kay stepped into the canoe, seating herself in the stern. Jerry leapt in after her.

"Taking the dog with you?" the man asked doubtfully.

"I don't like to leave him in the car."

"Well, you seem to know how to handle a canoe," said the man. "I guess you can manage all right."

Slowly Kay paddled away from the dock. Before she had taken a dozen strokes she saw that she would have trouble with Jerry. Apparently the dog had never been in a canoe before and the experience was proving to be an exciting one. He would not lie down. Instead he put his front paws on the upper edge of the craft and barked protestingly.

"Oh, Jerry, you're all right," Kay told him soothingly. "Lie down before you turn the boat over."

The dog might have become quiet but at that moment a wild duck landed on the water a short distance away. Instantly the animal made a dash to the other side of the canoe. The craft wobbled uncertainly, then before Kay could balance it, over it went.

"Jerry, for half a cent I'd give you to the dog catcher!" Kay spluttered as she came to the surface. "Of all the mean tricks!"

The river at this point was not deep, so Kay was able to wade ashore and tow the canoe after her. The dog swam along behind her, not at all disturbed by what he had done. When they reached the dock, he calmly shook himself and prepared to dry out in the sun.

"You were right about the canoe," Kay said ruefully to the man who had rented it to her. "With a dog like Jerry along, I need a flat bottom boat."

"Come into the office," he invited. "I'll build a fire and you can dry your clothes."

Within half an hour, Kay was ready to continue her journey down the river. Her clothing was dry again, but limp and wrinkled and she looked very messy.

"Better leave the dog here," the man advised as he launched a row boat for Kay.

The girl shook her head. "No, I'll take him along. I think he'll behave himself this time."

Jerry seemed to feel that he had done enough mischief for one afternoon. After barking a few times, he settled himself in the bottom of the boat and lost interest in his surroundings.

Since the current was fairly swift, rowing was easy. Within a short time Kay caught a glimpse of the Huntley mansion. From the river the grounds looked very imposing even in their ruined state.

Kay rowed quietly from cove to cove, protected from sight by tall bushes and willow trees which lined the banks of the stream. Slowly Kay drifted past the sunken garden. Some distance beyond she caught sight of an old boathouse which she had never noticed before. Once it had been a well-built structure, but now it was falling into ruin.

Resting on her oars, Kay studied the building with interest. It had been designed to harmonize with the old gazebo and the Japanese bridge. Windows on the upper storey had been broken, and several were stuffed with old rags.

"Someone must have lived in there recently," Kay thought in surprise.

She let the boat float nearer. Jerry, standing up, gave a little bark.

"Now don't become excited again," Kay said, reaching over to pat the animal. "If you start making a fuss, the Le Blancs will learn that we are here."

Paying no attention to her words, the dog barked louder than before. Kay noticed that he kept turning his head towards the boathouse as if something in that direction had excited him.

"What do you see, Jerry?"

Kay didn't see anything unusual, but as she listened intently she thought she heard a low moaning sound.

Quickly she steered the boat into a cove and tied it to a tree. Jerry leaped out. Before Kay could stop him he ran to the boathouse. Barking excitedly, he scratched against the front door with his paws.

"That moaning sound did come from there," Kay thought as she hurried towards the dog. "Someone must be in trouble!"

16

A Woman of Mystery

Reaching the boathouse, Kay quieted Jerry, then knocked on the door. There was no response. Now even the moaning sound had died away.

"I am sure someone must be here," she told herself. "Otherwise Jerry wouldn't act like this."

After knocking several times, Kay tested the door and found it locked. She turned away, only to pause as the dog began to bark again. He would scratch on the door, then gaze at Kay with pleading eyes.

"He doesn't want me to leave," the girl thought. "He's trying to tell me that someone is inside the place."

As she walked slowly around the boathouse, she found three windows on the lower floor, all of them shoulder height. From the river bank Kay brought an old log, placed it under one of the windows, and stood on it. In this way she was able to open the window. As she climbed through, Jerry barked so loudly that she was afraid he would disturb the Le Blancs. Quickly she opened the door and let him into the boathouse.

Immediately the dog ran up the stairway which led to the living quarters on the second floor. Kay followed as fast as she could.

On the top step she paused, amazed at what she saw. An emaciated woman of middle age lay on a cot. Her eyes closed, she seemed to be in a coma. Beside her sat Jerry, gazing worshipfully upon her face, his tongue gently licking the thin, white hand which hung limply over the bedside.

The woman aroused slightly and tried to pat the dog. Her eyelids fluttered open. With an effort she whispered, "You've come back at last. I thought they had killed you."

The hand fell back on the faded coverlet. Again the woman seemed to lapse into unconsciousness.

Kay moved to the bedside. She was shocked at the appearance of the woman. It was easy to see that hunger and pain had ravaged a face which once had been beautiful.

"Who can she be?" Kay wondered. "Jerry must be her dog, yet if he is, my theory that he belongs to Jane Barton is shattered."

Kay glanced around the room. Except for the cot, a cheap dresser, a table and two chairs, there was no furniture. Heat had been provided by a small stove, but there was no more wood. Looking into a cupboard, she found an empty coffee can and two slices of mouldy bread; nothing more.

"The woman is half starved," Kay thought, returning to the bedside. "I wonder if the Le Blancs know that she is living here?"

Remembering the basket of food which she had found in the gazebo, Kay decided that someone in the house must be aware of the woman's presence, and had made an effort to help her. Could that person have been Jane Barton?

After staring at the woman for a moment, Kay moved to the window and opened it to let in some fresh air. From the direction of the Huntley mansion she could hear the sound of piano music.

"The Le Blancs are having a rehearsal," she reflected. "Perhaps while they are occupied, I could slip into the house and get a little food for this poor woman."

Second thought convinced Kay that the plan would be too dangerous. It would be much wiser to take the boat and row to a nearby house, even if this would take longer.

Locking Jerry in the boathouse, she walked towards the

garden. It was just possible that a basket of food might have been left in the gazebo.

One glance assured her that the gazebo was empty, so again she went down to the river's edge. Remembering that she had noticed a house a short distance upstream, she rowed there. She made up a story and got a can of soup from the cook. As Kay carried the food back to the boathouse, it was growing dark.

Gathering wood, she built a little fire in the stove and heated the soup. When she carried the steaming broth to the bedside, the woman stirred and her eyelids fluttered open.

"Why did you leave me so long?" she mumbled fretfully. Her eyes were very blue and dull with pain.

Kay set down the bowl of soup on the table, and raised the woman to a sitting position. Carefully she supported her with pillows.

Dared she make a reply which would lead the woman to reveal more? It was fairly obvious that she had been mistaken for another person. Yes, she would attempt it.

"They tried to make me tell everything, but I refused," she said, pressing a spoonful of soup to the woman's lips.

The words seemed to make no impression upon the sick woman. Kay waited a moment, then added, "You must not stay here another day. You are very sick."

"You know I must remain, my child. And remember, no one must see me. You will not betray my secret?"

"No, it's safe with me," Kay replied soothingly.

After eating less than half the soup, the woman fell back against the pillows and dropped into a deep slumber.

"She may sleep for hours," Kay realized. "It is getting late, and if I don't return home Mother will be worried."

She didn't want to leave the woman alone but she realized she could do very little good by remaining. Deciding to return to Brantwood for help, she started down the stairway.

"Come, Jerry," she called.

The dog whined but refused to obey, even when Kay went back for him. Taking him by the collar, she attempted to lead him toward the stairway. He braced his feet and pulled away from her.

"You might as well stay here," she said aloud. "Guard your mistress until I come back, Jerry."

Letting herself out of the boathouse, Kay returned to the nearby cove. As she rowed upstream, she wondered about who the mysterious woman could be. Maybe she was Jane Barton's old lady companion whom Joe had mentioned.

"The woman isn't really old," she corrected herself. "I'll bet she's not a day over forty-five. If she were well, and her face filled out, she might be rather attractive again."

Suddenly a startling thought came into Kay's mind. The woman might be Jane Barton's mother, Trixie Rue!

"And perhaps she is the same person I saw dancing in the garden!" Kay reflected, becoming excited at the possibilities of her theory. "Mrs Cary told me that the woman was a professional dancer."

Although it was getting late, the girl didn't want to go home without trying to find out the identity of the mysterious woman. If only she could induce Mrs Cary to come back with her and see the person in the boathouse!

Upon reaching the dock, Kay asked the man in charge if she might use his telephone. Calling her mother, she explained that she would not be home for some time. She then inquired of the boatman how long his rental place would remain open.

"Please reserve a boat for me," Kay instructed as she hurried to her car. "I expect to be back again within an hour."

The attendent gave her a strange look, but didn't say anything.

Kay drove at once to Mrs Cary's cottage at the outskirts

of Brantwood. She found the old lady hobbling about the kitchen, preparing her supper.

"Well, well, this is a nice surprise," the woman said cordially. "You are just in time to have a cup of tea with me."

"No, I can't stay," Kay said quickly. "I came to ask a favour."

"I'll be glad to do anything I can for you. Is it sewing—"

"Nothing that easy, I fear. Would you be able to travel in a car and perhaps a boat?"

"A boat! You mean a steamship?"

"No, just a plain rowboat," Kay replied with a smile. "If you are able to make the trip, I should like to take you to the Huntley mansion—or rather to the boathouse on the grounds."

"But why should I go there?" Mrs Cary asked in confusion. "I'm feeling better than I did, but I haven't been out of the house in two weeks."

"I wouldn't ask, but this is an emergency."

"What's wrong at the Huntley place?"

"Do you remember telling me about a woman named Trixie Rue?"

"Yes, yes, of course!" Mrs Cary said eagerly. "You've not heard more about her?"

"I think I may have seen the woman this afternoon. Anyway, I visited the Huntley boathouse and found a poor creature living there. She is in a dreaful condition; ill and half starved."

"And you think she may be Trixie Rue!"

"Yes, the woman looks as if she might have been very beautiful at one time. I should say she is about forty-five years of age."

"Trixie Rue would be forty-six her next birthday," Mrs Cary murmured. "But I can't believe it! Mrs Huntley's sister starving—living in a boathouse!"

"I may be wrong, of couse," admitted Kay, "since I never saw Trixie Rue or even a picture of her. That's why I wish you could come with me and identify her. You would know the woman if you saw her again?"

"I'm sure I would, even if she has changed a great deal. If you will help me, I'll prepare a basket of food to take to the boathouse."

"Do you feel able to make the trip?" Kay asked anxiously.

Mrs Cary hesitated, then said with determination, "It will be an ordeal, but nothing could keep me from going. If Trixie Rue is ill and in trouble my place is at her bedside. We will start at once."

17

Old Friends

Mrs Cary packed a basket of food, and gathered up several blankets. The journey back to the river's edge was a tedious one. Kay drove slowly in order to spare the old lady unnecessary jolting. Even so the woman looked very tired by the time they reached the dock.

"How are you feeling?" Kay inquired as she helped her passenger from the car.

"A little tuckered out," Mrs Cary admitted. "But don't you worry about me. I'll make it all right."

The dockman gazed askance at Kay as she came to his shack to tell him that she was starting out again on the river. Noticing the lunch basket he figured she probably was going to attend an evening picnic somewhere along the shore.

"It's a pretty dark night to be in a boat," he said discouragingly. "Taking the old lady with you?"

"Yes, but we won't be gone long. I'll pay you for two hours' use of it in advance."

Pocketing the money, the man shrugged, and said no more. After Kay helped Mrs Cary into the boat, she wrapped a blanket about her to make her as comfortable as possible.

"My, but it is dark tonight," the old lady shuddered, staring down into the swirling waters.

"Later on I think we may have some light from the moon," said Kay.

"Are you a good hand at rowing?"

"Yes, you may trust me, Mrs Cary," the girl said reassuringly. "This boat is a very sturdy one, too."

"That's good," the woman replied, although even then she did not relax. "I hope it doesn't leak."

"Not a drop," laughed Kay.

As the girl rowed downstream, Mrs Cary sat tense and frightened, staring straight before her. After the first few minutes she did not speak. Kay was kept busy, for the swift current made the craft swing around time and again. As they approached the Huntley place, she noticed lights in the mansion windows. She pointed them out to her companion.

"It seems strange to see anyone living here after all these years," the woman said moodily.

"It will be better if we aren't seen," Kay cautioned, lowering her voice. "I'll try to row directly up to the boathouse. If I can get the big doors open we'll float inside."

She was able to manoeuvre into position. To her delight the doors rolled upward when she tugged at them.

"Someone is coming this way," Mrs Cary whispered suddenly.

As Kay turned her head, she caught a glimpse of a tall, lean figure moving swiftly toward the boathouse from the direction of the sunken garden. Although she was unable to see the man's face plainly she felt certain he must be Monsieur Le Blanc.

"I wonder if he heard us?" she thought tensely. "I don't see how he could have, but he's certainly coming right towards us."

Before Kay could swing the boat under the shed, the quiet of the night was broken by the muffled barking of a dog. The sound came from the upper floor of the boathouse. With a sinking heart the girl realized that Jerry had heard the approaching man and was trying to give an alarm!

"Now we will be caught," she thought in despair.

Monsieur Le Blanc, for indeed it was he, stopped short to listen. Then he gave an exclamation of anger and impatience. "There iss zat dog again! Never will I haff any peaze here. If I lay hands on him I drown him in ze river, *oui!*"

Satisfied that the dancing master had not realized that the barking was coming from the upper floor of the boathouse, Kay pulled the rowboat under the shelter of the building. She dared not lower the doors lest the noise give them away, but she felt fairly safe so far. If only she could quiet Jerry before he ruined all her plans!

"Mrs Cary, wait here," she whispered as she leaped out of the boat and made it fast. "I'll be right back."

Darting up the stairway she whistled softly to attract Jerry's attention. For an instant the dog stopped barking, then began again, louder than before.

"Quiet, Jerry!" she ordered sternly, grasping him by the collar.

Even then the dog would not obey. In desperation Kay covered his mouth with her skirt to smother the sounds. Jerry struggled violently to free himself, but she held on grimly.

Suddenly Monsieur Le Blanc pounded on the door of the boathouse. Kay held her breath.

"Iss anyone zere?" he shouted loudly.

Kay tightened her hold upon Jerry. If he should bark now all would be lost!

After a few minutes she heard Monsieur go away, muttering to himself. Still holding the dog, Kay moved to the window and watched until she saw the man disappear beyond the trees.

"Who is it?" asked the woman who was lying in darkness on the cot. "Who is there?"

"A friend," replied Kay softly. "Don't be alarmed. In just a moment we'll have a light."

"Pull down the shades first, please. They must not know I am here."

From the clear tone of voice Kay thought the woman must be feeling better. She wanted to ask her questions, but remembering that Mrs Cary was waiting patiently in the boat, Kay slipped quietly downstairs.

"Is it safe now?" the old lady whispered nervously.

"Yes, Monsieur Le Blanc has gone back to the house. We'll be all right if Jerry doesn't start barking again."

Taking Mrs Cary's hand, Kay led the woman up the creaking stairway.

"I have brought someone to see you," she said soothingly to the woman on the bed. "Just a minute until I get a light."

"There is one candle left. You will find it on the top shelf of the cupboard."

After lowering the blinds, Kay lighted the candle and placed it on the table. Mrs Cary bent over the woman on the cot. For several moments she stared but spoke no word. Then a little sob broke from her lips.

"Trixie—Trixie Rue!"

The patient stirred, trying to raise herself on an elbow.

"Is—it—Mrs Cary?" she asked in disbelief.

"Yes, yes, you remember me?"

"It was so—long ago," the woman muttered, sinking back on the pillow again. "So much has happened."

"What have they done to you, Trixie?"

"The world has battered my wings," the former dancer answered with a sad smile. "You—you shouldn't have come here, Mrs Cary. It may get you into trouble."

"Fiddlesticks!" snapped the old lady. "Now just set your mind at rest, Trixie Rue. From now on I'll be your nurse."

Thrilled that the missing dancer had been found, Kay began to unpack the lunch basket. She brought a dish of custard to the bedside, watching while Mrs Cary fed it to the woman.

"Now we don't dare give you too much at first, Trixie," the old lady said anxiously. "I can tell it's been a long while since you've had a good, square meal."

"So many days I can't remember," the dancer murmured, as a stray tear trickled down her furrowed cheek. "Oh, it's wonderful to be with friends again."

"You never should have run away from your trouble, Trixie."

"I know," the woman acknowledged, turning her head away.

Presently she ate a little more food and gazed at Kay with new interest.

"Who are you?" she asked wonderingly. "Weren't you here earlier this afternoon?"

"Yes, I think you mistook me for another person. My name is Kay Tracey."

"I did become confused," the woman admitted. "You look so much like my own darling Mary Jane."

"Your daughter?" Kay asked quickly. "Jane Barton?"

"Yes, my daughter. She has had such a difficult time—all my fault—oh, why was I born anyway?"

Burying her face in the pillow, the woman began to cry. Kay realized that she was in no condition to be questioned. She would have to wait until Trixie Rue was stronger before trying to learn her story.

Presently the dancer dropped into a peaceful sleep. Kay then took Mrs Cary aside to ask her opinion as to what should be done.

"We must get Trixie away from here," the old lady declared promptly. "This boathouse isn't a suitable place for a sick person."

"No, it is too damp and cold. Besides, Monsieur Le Blanc might take it into his head to investigate at any time."

"We ought to get her away from here tonight," insisted Mrs Cary.

"But where can we take her? Not to a hospital. We'd have to answer too many questions."

"She'll come to my cottage, of course," the old lady announced firmly.

"Will you be able to take care of her? You've not been very well yourself—"

"I'm getting better every day," Mrs Cary said spiritedly. "I'll be able to look after her all right."

"Then the next thing to do is convince the woman she must leave here. That may not be easy."

When Trixie Rue opened her eyes a few minutes later, the matter was presented to her. She listened thoughtfully and offered only one objection to the plan.

"If I leave here Mary Jane will not know where to find me again."

"Your daughter has been living in the Huntley mansion?" questioned Kay alertly.

"Yes, she often brought me baskets of food from there. The Le Blancs did not know about it. One day she left a basket for me in the gazebo, and another girl tried to take it. I had to slip up in the dark and jerk it away."

Kay smiled but did not reveal the fact that she had been the unknown person in the tea house. Aloud she said, "Perhaps we can get word to your daughter where we are taking you."

Trixie Rue shook her head. "Mary Jane must have been made to go away. If she were still here she would have come to her poor mother."

"If your daughter has gone, I can't see any possible reason for you to remain here," interposed Mrs Cary. "You will be more comfortable at my cottage."

"I'll try to find Mary Jane," Kay promised quickly.

"In that case, I'll be glad to go," said the former dancer. "It is dark and no one will see me."

After Mrs Cary and Kay had helped the woman get

dressed, they helped her downstairs to the boat. Jerry leapt in before they shoved off, settling himself comfortably at the feet of his mistress.

The boat rode so low in the water Kay found it hard work rowing. Her arms and back ached by the time they reached the dock. She hurried Trixie Rue and Mrs Cary to the car before the dockman had an opportunity to ask any questions.

"I hope he didn't see me," the dancer said nervously as Kay drove towards the Cary cottage. "If anyone should recognize me, it might mean a jail sentence."

"Why did you ever run away in the first place, Trixie?" Mrs Cary asked kindly.

"It's a long story, and I'm so tired. Tomorrow I'll tell you everything."

During the rest of the trip to the cottage, the dancer did not speak. She leaned her head against Mrs Cary's shoulder and slept.

At the cottage, Kay helped make Trixie Rue comfortable in the guest room. Secretly she was a little amused at the remarkable change in Mrs Cary's attitude toward her own ailments. In this emergency the old lady had forgotten about her invalidism, and rather resented any suggestion that she might be tiring herself out.

"Don't you worry at all about me," she assured Kay when the girl was ready to leave. "Trixie and I will get along fine."

"If you need anything let me know, Mrs Cary. I'll come back some time tomorrow."

Leaving Jerry at the cottage, Kay drove to her own home. The hour was late, she was hungry and very tired, but she felt that the evening had been a successful one. Not only had she helped poor Trixie Rue, but she had gained useful information regarding her double.

"When the woman is able to tell her story I'll find out a

lot more, too." she told herself triumphantly. "I only hope it doesn't turn out that Mary Jane Barton is involved in a dishonest scheme!"

As Kay approached the Tracey house, she saw a strange automobile drive away. Wondering who the visitor might have been, she drove into the garage and hurried to the house.

"Is that you, Kay?" called her mother from the living room.

"Yes, Mother. Was somebody here?"

Mrs Tracey waited until her daughter had reached the living room before she replied.

"Mr Trout was here again," she said, obviously upset. "He insists we pay damages at once or he will bring the case to trial without further delay."

18

Alarming Developments

"Tell me everything Mr Trout said," Kay demanded, sitting down beside her mother on the couch.

"He was very disagreeable and threatening. Not at all like he was the other day."

"I thought his smooth, polite manner was phony," Kay remarked grimly.

"He said if we would settle at once his client would accept three thousand dollars instead of five. I'm really worried, Kay."

Mrs Tracey got up and nervously paced the floor. Kay walked over and hugged her.

"Don't worry, Mother," she said. "We've already saved two thousand dollars by delaying, and if we keep waiting I don't think we'll have to pay anything."

"Oh, it isn't the money which worries me, although we can't afford to lose it."

"Then what's wrong, Mother?"

Mrs Tracey hesitated, then said reluctantly, "I'm worried about you, Kay."

"About *me?*"

"Mr Trout did not make any direct threats—he's too smart to do that—but he hinted something might happen to you if we didn't pay."

"He suggested I would be kidnapped?"

"I think he was implying that. Oh, if only Bill were here I wouldn't be so worried."

Kay thought quietly about Mr Trout's hints. And it really

was strange that they hadn't heard from Bill. It wasn't like him to stay away without letting either his relatives or his office know where he was. Oh, how she hoped nothing had happened to him! But she must not let her mother read her thoughts.

"I'm afraid Mr Trout is serious, Kay."

"Mother, you're not keeping anything from me, are you?"

Mrs Tracey didn't answer.

"You *are* hiding something from me! I can tell by the way you act."

"I didn't want to worry you," Mrs Tracey said slowly, "but I guess you really should know. For the past two days I've seen a stranger walking up and down in front of the house."

"You think he's watching us?"

"Yes, Kay, I do. Sometimes he stands across the street and at other times he hides in the alley."

"It couldn't be Mr Craken?" Kay asked thoughtfully.

"No, I would recognize him. This man is poorly dressed and I think he must have been hired to watch you. Now you understand why I feel uneasy."

"I'll be very cautious from now on, Mother," Kay promised, giving the woman a hug. "But I think you may be in more danger than I. You're here alone so much."

"Now don't start worrying about me," laughed Mrs Tracey. "I'm probably making a big thing out of nothing. By the way, aren't you going to ask me how many tickets I sold this afternoon?"

"Did you do well?" Kay questioned eagerly.

"Ten ladies promised me they will take tickets if you will stop by their homes. I could have sold more only it seems Chris Eaton has combed the town."

"Everywhere she goes, she spreads the word that our show is no good," Kay said bitterly. "It's very unfair of her."

"If I have a little spare time tomorrow, I'll try again," Mrs Tracey offered.

After thanking her mother for the help, Kay ate a late supper, then went to bed. She didn't sleep well. Once, thinking she heard footsteps in the driveway, she went to look out the window. She didn't see anyone, but she felt sure that someone had been prowling about the premises.

"If Bill were home he would do something to protect Mother while she's alone," she thought. "I should do the same."

Before she dropped off to sleep Kay decided to talk to Ronald's father about it in the morning. She left school at lunchtime and went to the factory building. Mr Earle, who had just returned from lunch, escorted her into his private office.

"Well, well," he said teasingly, offering her a chair, "aren't you playing hookey from school?"

"It's my lunch hour. I wouldn't have bothered you only I wanted to talk to you about something very important."

"What may I do for you, Kay?"

"First, I want to ask about Joe Kemp. Is he a good worker?"

"Exceptionally so, according to the report of my foreman. If you know of another young man like him, send him around."

"I was thinking of taking him away from you," Kay said with a smile.

She then told Mr Earle about the mysterious person who had been watching the Tracey house. Didn't he think the prowler should be watched also?

"A watchman to watch the watcher, eh?" Ronald's father chuckled.

"Yes, that's what I'd like to do, Mr Earle. Could you spare Joe from his work here?"

"You may have him if you like, Kay. I think he'll be

dependable, but I wouldn't trust him completely. You're not going to let him stay in your house, are you?"

"Oh, no. I really don't know him well at all."

"I'll call him now so you can talk to him."

In a few minutes Joe appeared at the office. He was wearing a clean suit, his hair was well combed, and there was a different look about his face which Kay noticed immediately.

"Did you send for me, Mr Earle?" he asked politely. "I—I hope my work has been all right."

"Entirely satisfactory. Sit down, Joe. Miss Tracey wants to talk with you."

Joe smiled as he noticed Kay was there. Without providing many details, she explained what she wanted him to do.

"I can't pay you very much," she finished regretfully. "And I can't tell how long the work will last."

"As far as your job here is concerned," said Mr Earle, "you may have it back again whenever you want."

"I'll be glad to work for you, Miss Tracey," Joe said immediately. "I'm not forgetting how much you've done for me."

"Great," said Kay. "I'd like you to start as soon as possible."

After thanking Mr Earle for his co-operation, Kay left the office. She decided not to tell her mother what she had done, realizing that it would make her more worried. She would pay Joe from her own savings account.

"Hi Kay, how was school?" Mrs Tracey asked as her daughter came in the living room.

"Fine, Mother. Let's go together to Mrs Cary's and talk with Trixie Rue. If she'll tell her story, everything may be cleared up."

Mrs Tracey packed a basket of food for the sick woman. Before Kay got in the car, she picked a large bouquet of flowers from their garden. It was just after two o'clock when the Traceys reached Mrs Cary's cottage.

Trixie Rue, looking much stronger than she had the day before, was sitting up in bed. She smiled at Kay, but responded somewhat coolly to Mrs Tracey.

"Mother won't tell anyone that you are here," Kay reassured the woman.

Even then Trixie Rue did not relax entirely. She seemed unwilling to talk about herself, despite her promise of the evening before. When she refused to talk about her past, Kay changed the subject to Mary Jane. The former dancer's face brightened and she began to speak more freely.

"Mary Jane is such a good, loyal daughter. All her life she has tried so hard to help me. Her courage has carried me on. We really were down and out when she saw Monsieur Le Blanc's advertisement in the paper."

"What advertisement was that?" Kay inquired, trying not to appear too eager.

"Monsieur is a dancing master," explained the woman. "He is training girls for a show, and has rehearsals at the Huntley mansion. Mary Jane was one of the twenty chosen."

"She must be very talented," said Mrs Tracey.

"Indeed, she is. I started training Mary Jane when she was four years old. Monsieur Le Blanc's show is below her level, but she couldn't get any other work and we were desperate."

"Does he pay his girls well?" Kay asked curiously.

"So far Mary Jane has received nothing except her room and board."

"Then she lives at the Huntley mansion?"

"She did stay there, but I don't know where they have taken her now. You see, Monsieur Le Blanc keeps his dancers in strict training, supervising their diet and sleeping habits. He overdoes it, in my opinion."

"The man seems to have very strong ideas about everything," Kay remarked.

"Yes, he is a hard master. I'm sorry Mary Jane had to work for him. He wouldn't let her keep Jerry. The dog stayed with me for a few days, then ran away to try to find Mary Jane. I didn't see him again until yesterday at the boathouse."

Now Kay was sure that Trixie Rue was the "old lady" whom Joe Kemp had seen living with Mary Jane in his apartment house. Maybe she had made herself up to look older than she was so nobody would recognize her.

"Mary Jane and I had been living in a fairly comfortable apartment, but I couldn't pay the rent. After my daughter went to the Huntley place, she sent for me. I lived in the boathouse without Monsieur Le Blanc's knowledge. At night Mary Jane would smuggle food to me. Then something went wrong. My daughter stopped coming, and I became ill."

"Do you think the man took his dancers to another place?"

"I don't know what to think. I'm sure Mary Jane would come to me if she were free to do so. Oh, please, will you try to find her for me?"

"I'll do anything I can," Kay promised. "Does your daughter have any friends who might know where she could be—a boy friend, perhaps?"

"There is no one, to my knowlege."

It was evident to Kay that Trixie Rue knew nothing of Hal Peterson or the recent car accident. For the time being she decided not to mention it.

"Maybe Jerry could help find your daughter," she said, looking at the dog. "Could I borrow him for a day or two?"

"Certainly. Jerry will go with you if I tell him he is to obey you."

"Do you have anything that belonged to your daughter? A scarf or a handkerchief?"

"I have a glove in my purse. It's lying on the bureau."

Kay got the glove, talked a few more minutes with Trixie Rue and returned home with her mother.

"If you can spare the car, I'll take Jerry and drive out to the Huntley estate," said Kay. "I may be able to learn something about Mary Jane."

At the mansion Kay knocked on the door several times. She could hear people moving around inside the house, but no one came to let her in. Refusing to be discouraged, she parked the car down the road and walked on to the grounds from the direction of the river.

Hiding herself in the sunken garden, she prepared to wait. Hours passed and Kay was getting very tired. Jerry became so restless it was difficult to keep him quiet.

As it got darker it became cold and chilly in the garden. Kay shivered, and thought about leaving. It didn't seem likely that she would get inside the mansion.

As she started to move away, the side door suddenly opened. Monsieur Le Blanc and his wife came into the garden. They didn't lock the door behind them, an oversight which Kay instantly noted.

"Here's our chance, Jerry," she whispered in the animal's ear.

Leading the dog by the collar, she stole to the door. Opening it softly she slipped into the house.

19

The Locked Door

Kay didn't think that she would find Mary Jane in the Huntley mansion, but she decided to make sure of this before searching elsewhere.

The lower floor of the house was dark. There was no indication that anyone was about. Taking Mary Jane's glove from her pocket, Kay dropped it at Jerry's feet. The dog sniffed at it and whined.

"Now find her!" Kay ordered, giving him an encouraging pat. "Find Mary Jane!"

With his nose close to the floor, the dog made little zig-zag patterns, rushing first in one direction and then in another. Each imaginary trail seemed to end about where it started. Finally Jerry stopped at Kay's feet, looking up at her as if to say, "This is confusing. Let me smell that glove again!"

Kay knelt down and held it close to the dog's nose.

"It's Mary Jane's, Jerry. Go find her!" she repeated.

This time the dog had better success. After running around a bit, he finally trotted over to a closed door on the first floor and began to whine.

"So you think you've found something interesting, do you?" Kay whispered as she reached for the knob. "Let's hope you're right."

Cautiously she opened the door and looked inside. It was a large, empty rehearsal room with mirrors lining the walls. Moonlight flooding in one of the windows lit up a large piano and a few sheets of music scattered on the floor.

"Try again, Jerry," Kay urged, leading the dog out into the hallway. "Mary Jane may have been here but she is gone now."

The animal acted as if he were a little mystified himself. Kay led him through the hall into the dining room. Here again she refreshed his memory by letting him sniff Mary Jane's glove.

This time Jerry ran to the foot of the stairway, going over every inch of the first step. Suddenly he placed both front feet on it and gazed up the stairway as if he were holding a secret debate with himself.

"So you think she is up there?" Kay murmured. "Well, let's try it."

She followed close behind as the dog bounded up the steps. In the upper hallway Jerry paused at each bedroom door and sniffed rather unconvincingly, as if he were following a very cold trail.

"You can't find her?" Kay whispered in disappointment. "Well, I didn't think she would be here."

On the lower floor the side door suddenly banged shut. Kay grasped the dog by his collar and flattened herself against the wall.

She heard the sound of footsteps as someone walked around downstairs. Her heart began to beat faster. It sounded like the person was a woman who wore high-heeled shoes; it was probably Madame Le Blanc.

Suddenly a creaking noise warned Kay that the person was climbing the stairs to the second floor. She must not be found!

Dragging Jerry by his collar, Kay opened a door which she thought led into a bedroom and pulled the dog in behind her. She found herself in a large linen closet which was lighted by a small window cut high in the wall.

Kay scarcely dared breathe as the woman reached the top of the stairway. Without glancing toward the linen closet, Madame Le Blanc went down the hall.

Jerry did not like being confined this way. He squirmed away from Kay. Before she could grab hold of him, his bushy tail brushed against an electric light bulb which had been left lying on top of a pile of linen. It crashed to the floor, exploding with a loud bang.

"Oh, now we'll be found for sure," Kay thought in panic.

The door of a bedroom was flung open as Madame Le Blanc rushed into the hallway. She switched on a light.

"What was that?" she called sharply. "Is anyone here?"

Kay remained perfectly still, hoping that she wouldn't be discovered. Jerry was trying to move around again. At any moment he might betray her with a bark!

To the girl's intense relief the woman did not seem to realize that the sound had come from the linen closet. She went down the hall in the opposite direction, opening and closing various bedroom doors.

Finally the woman gave up her search. She went downstairs where Kay could hear water running in the kitchen. A few minutes later the side door slammed shut, revealing that Madame Le Blanc had left the house. After waiting a little while to be certain the woman would not return, Kay came out of her hiding place.

"That was a close call, Jerry," she whispered in the dog's ear. "We'll try to go on with the search now, but please be more careful with that big tail of yours!"

Moving to a window at the end of the hall, she gazed down into the sunken garden. Madame Le Blanc had rejoined her husband. The two were strolling toward the gazebo.

Satisfied that the couple would remain outside for a while, Kay turned around to look for Jerry. The dog, having slipped away from her, was scratching on one of the doors. She hurried to open it for him.

To her surprise she discovered a flight of stairs. The dog bounded up the steps, Kay following as quickly as she could. The upper floor was just like the second floor—a long hall with several doors opening from it.

Jerry paused before one of them. He began to whine and stood on his hind legs, scratching to get inside.

"So you think Mary Jane is in there, do you?" Kay asked him softly. "You've made so many mistakes that I don't believe you."

She twisted the brass knob only to find the door locked.

"Is anyone there?" she called in a low voice.

Receiving no answer, Kay was satisfied that no one was inside.

Yet Jerry's actions were puzzling. When she turned away from the door, the dog stubbornly refused to follow. He kept scratching on the door and whining. Then he ran to Kay and tugged at her dress.

"Mary Jane couldn't be in there now or she would answer," Kay whispered to him patiently. "Come on, Jerry, before we get caught."

Grasping the dog by his collar, she dragged him away from the door by force. It has been a mistake bringing him to the house. He had been more of a nuisance than a help. If she didn't hurry away he might still give her away to the Le Blancs!

On the way to the stairs Kay passed a window. As she glanced down at the garden her attention was attracted by a moving object. She stopped suddenly and Jerry pulled away from her.

Dancing gracefully about in the moonlight was a white-robed figure. Surely the dancer could not be Madame Le Blanc or her husband trying out new steps and effects to be used in their stage show.

Kay dismissed the thought as quickly as it had come. Only a few minutes earlier she had seen the Le Blancs walking toward the opposite end of the garden, so it was doubtful that they were even aware of the dancing figure.

Completely forgetting Jerry, Kay opened the window and leaned far out over the ledge. She could hear someone singing. It was a man's voice and he carried the tune very poorly.

The dog, hearing the song, raised his front paws to the window sill and started barking loudly. The girl slammed down the window, but already Madame Le Blanc and her husband were running toward the house. The ghostly figure had disappeared in the darkness.

"Stop barking," Kay yelled angrily at Jerry. "You've ruined everything now!"

The animal would not be silenced. Suddenly the panicky girl realized why he was so excited. Above the noise she heard a girl's voice calling:

"Jerry! You've finally found me! I knew you would come to rescue me."

20

A Prisoner

Kay was so shocked that she forgot about her own danger. There was no doubt about it—the voice came from the locked room! The girl who was locked in there must have been asleep and the loud barks of the dog had wakened her.

"Jerry! Bring help," she pleaded.

Rushing to the door, Kay knocked to attract the attention of the person inside.

"Who is it?" she demanded in a whisper. "Are you Mary Jane Barton?"

"Yes, yes! They locked me in here and went away. Can you get me out?"

On the first floor a door slammed. Kay could hear Monsieur Le Blanc and his wife chattering angrily in French as they climbed the first stairway.

"There isn't time now," she told Mary Jane hurriedly. "The Le Blancs are on their way up here. Jerry and I will be caught too."

"Hide in the closet at the end of the hall."

"They'll search everywhere because they know the dog is here."

"Then if you have the courage to do it, climb out on the window ledge," Mary Jane instructed through the door. "It is wide enough if you balance yourself very carefully."

"The Le Blancs will be able to see me. I have on a light-coloured dress."

"There's a large black shawl in the closet at the end of the hall," Mary Jane said hurriedly. "Cover Jerry and yourself with that."

By this time the dancing master and his wife had reached the second floor. Kay found the shawl, dragged Jerry to the window and opened it.

As she looked down, she became even more frightened. The ledge was wide, so she could balance herself there easily, but to manage Jerry was a different story. If he refused to lie still, he easily could push them both to their deaths.

However, there was no time for thought. Quickly Kay scrambled over the sill. Pulling Jerry into her arms, she quietly lowered the window. When she dropped the shawl over the dog and herself, to her relief, he offered no resistance. Huddling close against the roof, she anxiously waited. A moment later the Le Blancs rushed up the stairway.

"Twice now I have heard the dog," Madame declared in a shrill voice. "Last night I thought it was nothing. Now I am sure there is a stranger in the house."

The couple searched diligently throughout the various attic bedrooms. Kay could not resist lifting a corner of the shawl to look at them, but she quickly lowered the cloth when the man turned his flashlight in her direction.

As he came toward the window, she remained perfectly still, holding Jerry in a tight grip. Her position now was a dangerous one. If the dog should move or make the slightest sound they would be caught.

"I find zis window unlocked again," she heard Monsieur say impatiently to his wife. "How many times haff I told you to be more careful?"

"I did lock it," his wife protested. "I remember doing so last night."

"Ze window is unlocked now—you see? Always you say, 'I do zis, I do zat,' but like all women your mind iss forgetful."

"Only the great Monsieur Le Blanc is perfect," the

woman retorted angrily. "Why do you not try doing a few things for yourself instead of expecting me to take care of everything?"

As they argued, the couple did not notice Kay huddled under the dark shawl. Suddenly her heart sank. The window latch was snapped into place.

She and Jerry were prisoners on the ledge!

After a few minutes Kay peaked from under the shawl. She saw that Monsieur Le Blanc and his wife were standing in front of Mary Jane Barton's room. The woman knocked sharply on the door.

"Mary Jane! Are you awake?"

"What is it?" the girl asked in a drowsy voice.

"If you are in bed, get up and put on your clothes. We wish to question you."

After a few minutes, Madame Le Blanc took a key from her pocket and fitted it into the lock. She and her husband entered the bedroom, closing the door behind them.

Kay wanted desperately to find out what was happening. She could hear an indistinct rumble of voices, but nothing more.

She looked around her. The wide ledge extended directly beneath the gently sloping roof. It would not be impossible to swing up on it and cross over to the window ledge under the window of Mary Jane's bedroom!

"Come on, Jerry," she whispered encouragingly. "Since we're locked out, we'll have to risk it sooner or later anyway."

Raising herself to the roof, she coaxed the dog up after her. A foot at a time she eased herself across the sloping roof and succeeded in reaching the other ledge without making any noise. Creeping along close to the wall of the building, she stopped herself by the window where she could see into Mary Jane's lighted bedroom. Kay was startled by what she saw.

"That girl does look enough like me to be my identical twin sister!" she realized.

Her double was sitting on the bed, staring at the floor. The Le Blancs were standing with their backs to the window.

"Now tell us ze truth, Mary Jane," the dancing master ordered angrily. "You hear someone on zis floor, yes?"

"I've been in bed for the past hour," the girl answered. "When you called, I woke up and got dressed."

"Surely you hear ze dog barking?"

"A dog?" Mary Jane asked innocently. "Are you sure? This isn't the first time that you have claimed you heard unusual sounds in the house, Monsieur Le Blanc."

"You are, what you call it—impertinent," the man said nastily. "Why I promise you a chance in my fine show I do not know. It was ze beeg mistake."

"You offered me a part because you know I am a good dancer," the girl replied with quiet confidence. "But I never would have accepted if I had suspected you would make me a prisoner."

"Then you should behave yourself," broke in Madame Le Blanc. "What good are you to us when you cannot dance?"

"My ankle will be better soon."

Suddenly Kay noticed that the girl's right foot was bandaged. It was evident that she had not recovered yet from the automobile accident. Apparently the Le Blancs did not know how the injury had been received for Madame said irritably, "I think maybe you only pretend to sprain the ankle, Mary Jane. You like to get out of practice."

"That isn't true," the girl argued. "I need the money badly. I must be in the show when it opens."

"Let me see you do your solo dance now," commanded the woman cruelly. "Then we will know if you pretend."

"Oh, please, not tonight," pleaded the girl. "I am so tired and—"

"Tonight! Now!" ordered Monsieur Le Blanc.

Mary Jane slowly got up from the bed. She began to dance, but as she made the first whirling turn, she suddenly collapsed with a moan of pain.

"Oh, my ankle! I've hurt it again. I shouldn't have tried to dance so soon."

"You will dance soon or not at all," Madame Le Blanc muttered without sympathy.

"Oui," added her husband grimly, "you do ze solo by tomorrow morning, or we, what you call it—keeck you out of ze show."

"You aren't giving me a fair chance," Mary Jane protested as she sank down on the bed again and began to cry. "How can I possibly do the dance by tomorrow morning?"

"Zat iss for you to decide," returned the master, shrugging his thin shoulders. "We will not feed you when you do not work."

Tears rolled down Mary Jane's cheeks. Unmoved, Madame Le Blanc and her husband turned to leave the bedroom.

"Please don't lock me in this hot, stuffy room again," the girl requested quickly. "If I could walk up and down the hall a few times I might be able to loosen the muscles of my ankle."

"If we let you out you would try to get away," Madame Le Blanc said, frowning.

"Why would I try to leave when I want to be in the show so badly?"

"Very well, you may walk up and down in the hall for a few minutes," the woman consented, pocketing the key. "We will wait until you have taken your exercise."

This didn't satisfy Mary Jane since she wanted to help Kay as soon as the couple left.

"Thank you," she murmured. "Could I have a glass of milk also? It is so hot up here under the roof. My head is throbbing."

"Always you want something," Madame Le Blanc complained bitterly. "The night is a cool one. But to keep you quiet I will get the milk."

She and her husband went down the stairway leaving Mary Jane a few minutes of freedom. The moment they had disappeared, the girl started toward the hall window.

"No, here I am, outside your room," Kay called softly, tapping the pane.

After hobbling back into the bedroom Mary Jane raised the window. As Kay leaped down from the ledge, the girl uttered a muffled scream.

"Who are you?" she gasped in surprise.

"Your double," Kay laughed. "It gave me a shock too when first I saw you."

"You must get downstairs right away," the dancer urged in a frightened voice. "Madame Le Blanc will be coming back here any moment."

"I can't go without you, Mary Jane. I came here to help you."

"There is a reason why I can't go," the girl answered sadly. "Please leave now while there is time. When Madame returns she will lock me in again."

"Not if my little scheme works," replied Kay mysteriously.

Kay ripped off a strip of cloth from her shirt and wadded it up. With a hairpin she pushed it into the door lock. She had just finished when the two girls heard footsteps on the stairway.

"She is coming!" warned Mary Jane in a terrified whisper. "Take Jerry and hide in the closet!"

Kay captured the dog and slipped out of sight an instant before Madame Le Blanc entered with the glass of milk.

"Here you are," she said to the dancer, setting the glass on the table. "What is the matter with you now? You are shaking like a leaf on a tree."

"I—I have a chill," the girl stammered.

"You will never be able to do the dance tomorrow," the woman said crossly. "It would be much better if you be put out of the show tonight."

"Oh, no, give me one more chance," pleaded the girl.

Madame Le Blanc waited until Mary Jane had drunk the milk. Then, taking the empty glass, she left the bedroom. She turned the key, but Kay, who listened closely, did not hear it click in the lock.

As soon as Madame Le Blanc's footsteps had died away, Kay came out of the closet. Darting to the door she tested it and found to her delight that it had not locked.

"We can escape very easily now, Mary Jane," she said excitedly. "I thought my little scheme might work!"

"I wish I could go with you, but I can't. There is a reason why I have to stay—someone is depending upon me—"

"Your mother?" asked Kay.

"How did you know?"

"Because I found her living in the boathouse down by the river. She was sick and hungry."

"Oh, my poor mother."

"I took her to the home of an old friend," Kay explained reassuringly. "She is being well cared for by a Mrs Cary."

"I've been so worried about her," confessed Mary Jane in a calmer voice. "I couldn't go to her because they locked me up in this attic room."

"Why?"

"Madame Le Blanc caught me stealing food. It was for Mother, but she thought I intended it for myself, and Monsieur is very strict about a dancer's diet."

"Still, it was cruel to keep you up here."

"Monsieur Le Blanc was especially angry at me because I hurt my ankle. He thinks I sprained it, but the truth is, I twisted a tendon in a car accident."

"I know, Mary Jane."

"You *know*?" the girl said in surprise. "How could you? I just met you a few minutes ago!"

"I am being sued for your accident," Kay explained unhappily. "A Mr Craken demands that I pay him three thousand dollars. Since we look so much alike, others have mistaken us for the same person. Everything is in a mix-up."

"It was a bad accident," Mary Jane worried. "Still, I didn't think he'd try to sue me. Now I'm in worse trouble than before."

"So far I'm the one who is being sued," chuckled Kay. "Don't worry about that right now."

Jerry had been lying at Mary Jane's feet, licking her hand. Now he suddenly pricked up his ears and listened.

"Sh!" Kay warned alertly. "I think someone is sneaking up the stairs."

"It's probably Madame Le Blanc again! What should we do?"

"Jump into bed and pull the covers over you," Kay said as she turned off the light. "Pretend to be asleep."

"I'll take care of Jerry," Mary Jane offered, grabbing the dog. "He'll be much quieter with me."

Kay intended to hide in the closet again, but she had waited too long. There was no time in which to cross the room. She barely had a moment to roll under the bed before Madame Le Blanc reached the top step. The woman turned the key, thinking that she had unlocked the bedroom door. She entered quietly.

"Are you asleep?" she called in a whisper.

When there was no answer she tiptoed across the room to stand by the bedside and look intently at Mary Jane.

21

Trixie Rue

The moment was a tense one for both Mary Jane and Kay. Any second Jerry could give them away by moving under the covers. Finally, Madame Le Blanc seemed satisfied that the girl was asleep and she tiptoed out of the room.

Neither of the girls heard her go down the steps so for over a half hour they remained still, afraid to move a muscle in case the woman was listening at the door. At last Kay could endure the cramped position no longer. Deciding that Madame Le Blanc must have gone to a lower floor, she cautiously whispered, "Mary Jane."

"Yes?"

"Do we dare turn on a light?"

"It would be dangerous. Madame may be hiding in the next room. She is very sneaky."

"I can't stand it here much longer," Kay complained, stretching a stiff arm. "We ought to get out while the coast is clear."

"I can't leave," Mary Jane protested, still whispering. "If you knew everything—"

"Tell me your story, Mary Jane. In the first place, how did you happen to be in a car accident?"

"I borrowed a car which belonged to Madame Le Blanc's brother," the girl admitted reluctantly. "It hadn't been used for some time because Lazzare is in Europe."

"You didn't ask the Madame's permission?"

"No. She had said that none of the girls were to leave the house, but I just had to get away for a little while. Everything would have been all right if only I hadn't crashed into that other car."

"How did the accident happen, Mary Jane?"

"It wasn't my fault—I'm sure it wasn't. I was driving along at a moderate speed when a car swerved so that I couldn't avoid hitting it. It seemed like the driver did it on purpose!"

"You may be right," Kay commented softly.

"The car was an old wreck and looked as if it had been in a lot of accidents," Mary Jane went on, "but I didn't think about that at the time. I guess the crash must have stunned me. Anyway I woke up in the hospital with a twisted ankle and a few bruises."

Kay was very interested in the story. Convinced that Madame Le Blanc would not return without them hearing her come, the girl rolled from under the bed and sat down beside Mary Jane.

"I guess you didn't give the hospital authorities your real name?" she questioned the girl.

"Yes, I did!" Mary Jane declared. "I assure you, I had no intention of being a hit-and-run driver even if the accident wasn't my fault. I not only gave my name but my address as well."

"The police came to see you at the hospital?"

"No, because I left right away. I thought they might talk with me later, but they didn't. That's why I figured I wouldn't get into any trouble on account of the accident."

"What happened to the car, Mary Jane?"

"You mean the one I borrowed? I think the police must have towed it away. It was never returned here. Madame Le Blancs thinks it has been stolen and I haven't the courage to tell her the truth."

"You are in an awkward position," said Kay.

"It's worse than awkward," sighed Mary Jane, restraining Jerry who was trying to jump off the bed. "They can't sue me for any money because I don't have a dime, but the police might send me to jail. Then what would become of my poor mother?"

"You would do almost anything for her, wouldn't you, Mary Jane?"

"Yes," the girl answered simply. "If it weren't for her I would give myself up to the police. But you must understand. She needs me to support her, and all her life she has counted upon me becoming a great dancer."

"Your mother was also a talented dancer?" questioned Kay, hoping that Mary Jane would reveal some facts about her family.

"Mother trained me," she replied, offering no additional information.

Kay was a little annoyed for it was obvious that Mary Jane had no intention of telling anything about her mother's past. If the girl didn't confide in her, she would not be able to help her out of her present situation.

"Mary Jane, I wish you would tell me why your mother must remain in hiding," she urged. "I might be able to help you both if only you could bring yourself to trust me."

"How could you help?"

"For one thing, I might be able to save your place in the show. I dance fairly well, and we look enough alike to fool almost anyone."

"But why would you want to help me?" the girl asked somewhat suspiciously. "You don't know me at all, and I've already caused you a lot of trouble."

"You and your mother need a friend."

"Yes, we do," Mary Jane acknowledged, torn between emotions. "I—I don't know what to say—"

As if sensing her uncertainty, Jerry began to lick the hand of his mistress. He then crawled across the bed and licked Kay the same way.

"Jerry is trying to tell me that you are my good friend as

well as my double," laughed Mary Jane softly. "And I think he's right."

"Mother's story is an upsetting one," the dancer began slowly. "I suppose you have heard that we were related to the Huntleys who once occupied this home?"

Kay nodded.

"Mother's first husband—my father—was gassed in the War and died a few years later. His name was Barton, so naturally I call myself Mary Jane Barton."

"But your mother is Trixie Rue?"

"After my father's death she married again," explained Mary Jane, a note of bitterness creeping into her voice. "My stepfather was a talented dancer, but a selfish, cruel man. He used mother's money, deserted her, and left our business affairs in a terrible mess."

"Why didn't Mrs Huntley help?"

"Oh, she did," Mary Jane answered quickly. "Even before my stepfather left she gave Mother money. Then later she tried to set her up in business, lending her several thousand dollars. The problem was that Mother had bad judgement regarding people. She trusted a man who turned out to be a con-man. They went into partnership together. Later she was told that in the name of the firm he had signed bad cheques which would send them both to jail.

"Mother panicked. She fled to Europe, taking me with her. The matter was hushed up, and as soon as possible Mr and Mrs Huntley went abroad also. After Mr Huntley's death, Mother and I lived very happily in Paris with my aunt. I studied dancing, we visited the art galleries and were very comfortable. But it lasted only a short time."

"Mrs Huntley died?" Kay asked sympathetically.

"Yes, she had a heart attack and passed away very suddenly. It was a shock to us when we learned about her will. My aunt always said that she had left everything to Mother and me, but we didn't receive a penny. The lawyers told us that everything was left to charity."

"Strange, when Mrs Huntley cared so much about your mother," Kay remarked thoughtfully. "Did you see the will?"

"I believe the lawyers showed a paper of some sort to Mother."

"She was satisfied that her sister had cut her off without a penny?"

"No, she wasn't," Mary Jane declared. "Mother always said she thought the lawyers cheated us, but we had no proof. We couldn't do anything. It would have taken money to contest the will, and we had barely enough to get back to the United States."

"I would think your mother would have been afraid to return to this country considering the charge against her."

"We had no choice because neither of us could find work abroad. Mother disguised herself as an old lady. For a while we lived in a cheap furnished apartment but we used up all our money."

"Oh, now I understand why Joe thought your mother was an old woman," Kay murmured to herself.

"Joe?" inquired Mary Jane in surprise. "Do you know Joe Kemp?"

"He's working for me now," Kay returned, smiling.

"I never knew him very well," Mary Jane admitted. "Mother and I often noticed him in the apartment house, but we avoided talking with him for fear he would find out about us."

"I do know a good friend of yours. His name is Hal Peterson!"

"Oh, do you really know *him?*" asked Mary Jane eagerly.

"He thought I was you, and I had a very interesting evening."

"Hal came here to the house to see Monsieur Le Blanc," Mary Jane revealed in a dreamy voice. "He was an agent for the advertising firm which will handle publicity for our show. We met by accident in the hallway and—"

"A case of love at first sight?" Kay interrupted teasingly.

"Well, practically so," admitted Mary Jane, laughing self-consciously. "Hal kept making excuses to call at the house, and one evening he brought several young men, fairly prominent in the theatrical world. The Le Blancs were almost forced to give a party and allow all of us to attend, but were they angry! Madame Le Blanc hates to waste a penny, especially for food."

"I bet Hal brought his friends just to get to see you again, Mary Jane."

"I thought so at the time," the girl admitted softly. "He said he would call again, but he never did. I guess I was silly to allow myself to become interested in him."

"Mary Jane, Hal Peterson is very much in love with you."

"Really in love with me?" the girl whispered, gripping Kay's hand. "Oh, it would make me so happy! But how could you say such a thing! You don't know how he feels toward me."

"But I do, Mary Jane. Hal Peterson is eager to marry you whenever you say the word. He told me so."

"He told *you!* Why doesn't he tell me about it?"

"He has us hopelessly mixed up," Kay laughed. "I met him in a restaurant and he thought I was you. I admit I should have told him my real name, but I didn't. He proposed to me and I have a date with him for Saturday night. Or rather you have!"

"This doesn't make any sense."

Kay gave a more detailed account of her meeting with Hal Peterson, and ended by insisting that Mary Jane must keep the Saturday evening date with the young man.

"I wouldn't know what to tell him," Mary Jane replied unhappily. "How can I agree to marry Hal when Mother depends upon me? I have to pursue my career."

"You're sure you want to be in the show?"

"It will be a step upward. If my dancing attracts attention, I should be able to get better work."

"Do you think you will be able to do your solo dance by tomorrow morning?"

"My ankle hurts me terribly," she answered. "I'm afraid I'll do terribly, but I have to try."

"But you might permanently injure your foot so you'll never be able to dance again."

"The doctor did warn me to be careful," Mary Jane admitted anxiously. "But unless I try out for the part tomorrow, I'll lose my chance to be in the show."

Kay was silent for a moment. She really wanted to help Mary Jane. Besides, she was excited by the information the girl had revealed about her mother's past. By staying at the Huntley Mansion she might find some more information which might help her solve the case.

"Mary Jane, there's only one thing to do," she said decisively. "We must change places. You can return to my home while I stay here and try to win a place for you in the show!"

"The Le Blancs would be sure to realize you're not me," said the girl nervously.

"Not if you teach me the steps of your solo dance."

"I can't do it here," Mary Jane protested. "Madame Le Blanc would hear you practising."

"We'll slip outside and rehearse in the garden!" Kay suggested. "Come on, there's no time to lose!"

22

Rehearsal by Moonlight

Against her better judgment, Mary Jane Barton allowed Kay to convince her that the scheme would work, though she didn't think she should stay at Kay's house.

"Mother will be glad to have you," Kay assured her new friend. "I'll write her a note. She's very understanding."

Mary Jane got a pen and paper. Kay wrote a quick message and then tried on the older girl's dancing shoes and costumes. Everything fitted perfectly.

"We really are duplicates in almost every way, Mary Jane," she laughed. "I only hope I can dance half as well as you."

"Monsieur Le Blanc is an expert," Mary Jane replied uneasily. "It's really going to be hard to fool him."

"Well, let's get started then."

Taking Jerry with them, the two girls cautiously stole down the stairway and into the garden. The lower part of the house was entirely dark, so they figured that the Le Blancs had gone to bed.

They found a level piece of ground and Mary Jane hobbled through her dance as best she could. Kay watched closely, asking questions about the more difficult steps which the girl could not demonstrate because of her injured ankle.

"Now you try the first movement," Mary Jane suggested. "I really am afraid it will prove too difficult for you."

Kay said nothing, but began to dance with confidence, going through each step almost perfectly. Mary Jane was amazed.

"Why, you do it beautifully," she said as she applauded. "One would think you had practised the routine for months!"

"Many of the steps are familiar," Kay laughed, proud of how well she'd done. "Our school dance club is presenting a show next week at the Children's Home. In one of our numbers we use a solo very much like yours."

"You really dance like a professional," Mary Jane said enthusiastically. "I must admit that I didn't really think you could pull it off."

"Now you think I can?" asked Kay excitedy.

"Yes, I'll drill you a little more to be certain. Even one mistake infuriates Monsieur Le Blanc. He is so temperamental."

"You have it perfectly," Mary Jane said after they practiced a while longer. "Let's rest for a few minutes."

While Kay sat down on a stone bench to catch her breath she listened to a detailed account of Monsieur Le Blanc's rehearsal routine. Mary Jane told her the position she would occupy in the chorus, and the names of the girls she would meet, giving a brief description of each person.

"Elaine Carson may talk to you, but the others have never been very friendly," she remarked. "You'll have no trouble deceiving them."

"Do the girls live in the house?" Kay asked curiously.

"A few of them do. They were all here for a while, but Monsieur Le Blanc decided he couldn't afford it any more. Remember, rehearsals start promptly at eight-thirty."

"I think I have everything straight," replied Kay, standing up. "Oh, one more thing. You'll go meet Hal Peterson Saturday night?"

"Yes, but I can't promise to marry him. I have to continue dancing."

"Would you feel differently if your mother had enough money to live on?"

"I might. But why think about the impossible?"

"You never know what can happen, Mary Jane. I have a feeling that things may work out better than you hope. Let's not talk about that now. The point I meant to bring up is this: if you see Hal, you must act as if you had met him last Tuesday night."

"Don't worry, I will," promised Mary Jane, laughing for the first time.

As the girls and Jerry walked to the car, Kay told Mary Jane how to reach the Tracey home. She also promised that she would try to write a note the next day and hide it near the road where Mary Jane could pick it up.

"You're not afraid to drive, are you, Mary Jane?" she asked.

"I do feel a little nervous after such a disastrous accident," the girl admitted. "But I'll get there all right."

The two girls said good-bye, wishing each other luck. Mary Jane drove away with Jerry. It was an easy car to drive, but her ankle hurt badly whenever it was necessary for her to step on the brake. After turning down several wrong streets, she finally located the address given her by Kay. Somewhat timidly, she introduced herself to Mrs Tracey.

"My goodness, for a moment I really thought you were my daughter!" the woman exclaimed in astonishment. "Come in, Mary Jane."

"I have a note from Kay, Mrs Tracey. It explains everything."

The message asked Mrs Tracey to let Mary Jane stay at the house until Kay returned from the Huntley mansion. If possible she was to keep the dancer's identity a secret.

Although she was very upset her daughter was staying overnight at the mansion, Mrs Tracey tried to hide her uneasiness. She assured Mary Jane that she was welcome to stay as long as she wanted to.

"I won't trouble you except for tonight," the girl said, as she explained how Kay hoped to save her place in the show.

"My dear child, surely you don't expect to dance very soon with that injured ankle!"

"I have to," Mary Jane replied seriously. "Don't you think it will be better in a day or so?"

"Only a doctor could tell you that."

"I was supposed to have gone back to Doctor Brown the day before yesterday, but I couldn't get away from the Huntley mansion."

"It is very foolish to neglect an injury," Mrs Tracey said. "I think we should call a doctor immediately."

"I guess you're right," the girl agreed reluctantly. "You're very kind."

Mrs Tracey knew that Doctor Brown was aware of Mary Jane's amazing resemblance to Kay, so after a moment's though she decided to call in a specialist who had never seen either of the girls. When Doctor Farnsdale arrived a half hour later, he assumed that the patient was Mrs Tracey's daughter.

"This ankle has been neglected, young lady," he said severely, after he examined it. "My orders are to keep off it for three days."

"But Doctor—"

"If you refuse to follow my instructions, I can do nothing for you. I'll massage the ankle and rebandage it, but unless you give the muscles and tendons an absolute rest, there will be no improvement."

"If I do keep off it will I be able to dance within three or four days?"

"So you are a dancer?" the doctor smiled. "I remember reading about the show in the paper last night. A benefit for the new Children's Home, isn't it? A very worthy cause."

Neither Mary Jane nor Mrs Tracey replied, but the doctor did not notice this, for he was taking adhesive tape and bandages from his black case.

"We'll have to get you patched up by that time," he laughed. "Yes, I'll promise that if you'll give your ankle an absolute rest you'll be able to dance again within four days."

When he finished his work, he again warned Mary Jane to be careful, then he left. As Mrs. Tracey went to the front door with the doctor, she noticed Joe Kemp standing across the street. Recognizing him as the young man whom Kay had helped to find work, she wondered why he was there.

Switching off the light, she stood for a long time at the window. Finally Joe wandered slowly down the street. With a sigh of relief, Mrs Tracey went upstairs with her guest and they went to bed.

In the morning while Kay's mother was preparing breakfast, there was a knock on the kitchen door. Opening the door, she was surprised to see Joe Kemp standing on the porch, his eyes bloodshot from lack of sleep.

"May I see Miss Tracey, please?" he requested in a tired voice.

"Why, Kay isn't here now," Mrs Tracey said without stopping to think about it.

Joe gave the woman a strange look.

"She isn't here? I just saw your daughter through an upstairs window!"

"Oh!" Mrs Tracey became flustered. "I mean that she can't have any visitors."

"Your daughter isn't sick, is she?" Joe asked quickly. "I saw the doctor leaving the house last night."

"I called in a specialist to look at an ankle that was hurt in an accident," the woman said nervously.

"Say, that's too bad," Joe replied sympathetically. "You think I can't talk with her?"

"Not today, I'm afraid."

"I don't know what to do. She told me to report if I found out anything about that man who has been watching your house."

"I wondered why you were standing across the street last night. Why don't you tell me what you found out."

"There's no reason for you to worry, Mrs Tracey, I've found out that the man is a private detective. He was sent to guard the house."

"Well, of all things!" exclaimed Mrs Tracey, sighing in relief. "By whom, I wonder?"

"I haven't been able to find out yet."

Mrs Tracey thought that she could guess. Surely Bill had been responsible for hiring the detective. Even though he hadn't let anyone know where he was he had kept in touch with the situation.

After Kay's mother promised to deliver Joe's message, the young man left the house without realizing that the girl he had seen through the window actually was Mary Jane. One his way back to the rooming house where he lived, he met Mr Earle. The man stopped to inquire how he was getting along with his new work for Kay. During the conversation Joe mentioned that Kay had sprained her ankle severely in an accident.

Later that morning Mr Earle told this to Ronald, who in turn told Wendy and Betty Worth. By afternoon Chris Eaton had heard about it too. She was the only person who received the information with elation.

"I guess Kay won't be able to dance in the show now!" she smiled to herself. "And the other members of the club will dance to empty seats! It serves them right for not letting me join."

Unaware of the story being told about her accident, Kay was having an exciting and busy day at the Huntley mansion. It started early in the morning when she was awakened by a loud pounding on her bedroom door.

"Mary Jane!" called Madame Le Blanc in a shrill voice. "Get up!"

A key turned in the lock but, as Kay knew, the door had not been locked.

"Rehearsals in twenty minutes!" the woman warned her without coming into the bedroom. "Remember, if you fail this time, out you go!"

Kay rushed to put on the costume which Mary Jane had laid out for her. She combed her hair the way Mary Jane did and then tried a few of the dance steps to refresh her memory.

"Now I guess I'm ready," she thought. "Oh, I nearly forgot to bandage my ankle!"

She quickly wrapped the tape around her ankle and ran down the stairway. At the door of the rehearsal room she hesitated to gather courage.

"I can't fail," she whispered to herself. "It's going to be difficult, but for Mary Jane's sake I have to do my best."

23

A Revealing Conversation

Opening the door, Kay walked slowly into the rehearsal room. She had a moment of panic when she saw several other members of the dancing troupe there ahead of her. Except for a few sleepy "good mornings" the girls ignored her. Limping slightly, she went over to a chair against the wall and sat down.

"Monsieur isn't here yet?" she asked a dark-haired girl who was adjusting ribbons on her toe shoes.

"No," she replied without glancing up. "*He* has a fit if *we* are a minute late. It's all right for him to oversleep."

Now Kay knew that her voice would not give her away.

"Here he comes now!" her companion exclaimed, rising quickly to her feet.

As Monsieur Le Blanc entered the room the girls lined up across the floor. The dancing master's alert gaze swept from one person to another, rested for an instant upon Kay, then went on.

"We will do our setting up exercises now," he announced sharply. "Mademoiselle Elaine—you at ze end. Up shoulders! Music! Now, *une, deux, trois!*"

The man's nasal voice droned on, counting monotonously as the girls twisted, bent and stretched in time to the music. Kay had no difficulty in following the movements of the others since she had practised similar exercises at school.

"Now to breakfast!" ordered Monsieur Le Blanc after fifteen minutes of strenuous work. "A leetle rest and then back here at nine o'clock. Plenty of work today."

The girls who lived in the mansion trooped into the dining room. Kay waited until everyone had found a seat, then slid into the one empty chair.

"Monsieur Le Blanc has his nerve to call this meal a breakfast!" said one of the dancers angrily. "What does he think we are anyway? Humming birds? Nothing to eat except dry toast and cold cereal."

"And skimmed milk," added another girl. "He gives us less to eat each day and works us harder."

Even if the food had been good Kay could not have eaten very much because she was very nervous. She had fooled everyone so far, but the most important test would come when she danced alone.

"Don't you ever answer when your name is called, Mary Jane?" demanded a voice at her right.

Apologizing, Kay turned around to face a dreamy-eyed girl who reminded her of Wendy Worth. She saw that she was the same dancer whom Monsieur Le Blanc had called Elaine.

"You're not eating very much this morning," the girl observed.

"No, I'm not very hungry."

"Well, you look as if you felt better than you did yesterday, Mary Jane. Your eyes have their old sparkle."

"Thank you," laughed Kay.

"It's the effect of love, no doubt. Have you heard from Hal yet?"

"Perhaps," replied Kay with a smile, and began to eat her cereal.

Breakfast finished, the girls were allowed a few minutes of freedom. Kay went upstairs to her room and started to make the bed. While she was leaning over with her back to the door a woman carrying a dust cloth and a mop quietly entered the room. When she saw Kay she dropped them and screamed, "Mercy on us!"

Startled Kay whirled about, thinking that the maid had realized that she wasn't Mary Jane.

"You shouldn't have done that, Mary Jane! It's bound to bring you bad luck!"

"What will bring me bad luck?" Kay asked, recovering from her fright.

"Why, removing your mole, Mary Jane! Just before the show opens, too."

"Oh, I'm not superstitious," laughed Kay. "You must admit I did a good job in taking it off. I'll bet you can't even tell where it was!"

"I can too," the cleaning woman insisted. "It was on the back of your neck."

"About here?" inquired Kay, pointing with her finger.

"No, about an inch lower down."

"Even if you know where it was, you can't see the scar," chuckled Kay.

When the cleaning woman had gone, Kay took Mary Jane's make-up box and painted a small black spot on the back of her neck. As she was putting away the kit, there was a knock on the door. Before she could answer, it was pushed open by one of the girls, a tap dancer whom Kay had heard the others call Susie.

"You're wanted down in the rehearsal room, Mary Jane. Monsieur Le Blanc says you're to come immediately. You must do your solo or else—"

"Or else I be keecked out of ze show?" Kay asked, mimicking the dancing master's speech.

"It might be worse than that," hinted Susie. "The great Monsieur says he may turn you over to the police."

"He can't be serious!" Kay said in surprise.

"That man never makes joke. He think you've been stealing food—oh, yes, and an automobile!"

This upset Kay, since she knew that Mary Jane thought

the Le Blancs didn't realize that she had anything to do with the missing car. If Monsieur had known about it all this time, why hadn't he confronted her before?

"If you're able to do your solo dance well, I think he'll be fairly lenient with you," Susie said as she turned away. "He really needs you in the show, Mary Jane."

"I'll be right down, Susie."

After the girl had gone, Kay again ran through a few of the steps of the dance to refresh her memory. Then she gave her hair a quick brushing in front of the mirror and rushed to the rehearsal room. As Kay entered, the master gave her a hard, cold smile.

"You are ready, Mademoiselle?"

"Yes, Monsieur Le Blanc."

"Let us hope my little one will not fail," the man said with a smirk. "It would be—ah, what you say—tragic beeziness to see one so young, so charming, so bee-u-tiful, in ze jail."

Luckily, the music started at this moment. Kay put all her effort into the number. Now and then she caught a glimpse of the master's face and was sure that he felt satisfied with the performance.

"Um, zat iss good," he praised grudgingly when she had finished. "Later we will perfect some parts. You caught ze rhythm. And now since ze ankle is well again, I will put you in ze ensembles."

Kay panicked; she was unfamiliar with any of these routines. Mary Jane had taught her only a few of the steps, thinking that she would not be asked to do more than the solo number.

"Monsieur," she pleaded, sinking down into a chair. "Not today. My ankle still pains me, and I should give it a rest."

"Line up with ze others or out you go!" the man cried in sudden fury. "You are lazy, zat is ze trouble!" Kay nervously limped away to join the other girls. So far she had escaped detection, but now she didn't know how she could get away with it. Her one hope was Elaine.

When she found her, Kay asked, "Would you mind running over the steps with me? I haven't tried them for so many days I'm terribly rusty."

Elaine looked at her in surprise.

"I didn't know you ever forget a step, Mary Jane. Come out into the hall, and we'll go over them together. But we have only a minute."

As they practised together, Kay asked a lot of questions, learning her position in the line-up and just what would be expected of her.

"My, you have forgotten a lot," Elaine said as they joined the others. "But with luck you should get by."

Luck was with Kay. She watched the others carefully during the rehearsal and made only one mistake. Fortunately Monsieur Le Blanc did not see it. However, the session was very difficult for Kay and she was more than ready for the brief rest period when it finally came.

"Now to your rooms for half an hour," ordered the harsh master. "We practise again at eleven."

Madame Le Blanc, who had been watching the rehearsal, stood and spoke to her husband as the girls filed out of the room.

"I go now to make a telephone call, Henri. If you will excuse me, please?"

"*Très bien,*" the man replied irritably. "But do not be long."

Kay lingered behind after the other girls had gone upstairs. She saw Madame Le Blanc go to a small study next to the dining room. Carefully the woman closed all the doors.

"I wonder who she's calling," thought Kay. "It must be an important conversation or she wouldn't be so afraid someone might hear it.

The lower floor seemed deserted, for the dancing master

had stayed in the rehearsal room. Kay tiptoed to the doorway of the study.

"Hello, hello, is this you, Lazarre?" she heard Madame Le Blanc ask in a low voice.

The name startled Kay, who had been under the impression that the woman's brother was abroad. Had he returned to Brantwood recently? Now deeply interested in the telephone conversation, she pressed her ear close to the door.

"Nothing new has developed," she heard Madame say. "What is that, Lazarre? But it cannot be true! Trixie Rue is dead! She could not be here in this country!"

Apparently the man at the other end of the wire convinced his sister that the information was correct, for in a moment Kay heard her moan, "This is terrible, Lazarre. Does she suspect anything?"

Kay could only guess at the response which she thought must have been in the negative. She listened intently as Madame Le Blanc went on.

"How will you find her, Lazarre? We have not one single clue."

There was a long pause, then Madame said in amazement, "Why, Lazarre, I never even thought of that before! The girl we have here, Mary Jane, may be the daughter of Trixie Rue! I find out at once!"

Kay heard nothing else, because at that moment a door at the end of the hall opened. Frantically she looked about for a place to hide.

24

Final Clues

Barely in time to avoid being seen, Kay ducked into the dining room. Peeking through a crack in the door, she saw the cleaning woman come down the hallway with her mop and broom.

"No chance of hearing any more now," Kay thought in disappointment. "But later I have to get into the study and look around."

She was convinced from the phone conversation that Lazarre had played an important part in Trixie Rue's life. Also, she remembered hearing Monsieur say that his wife's brother had got money dishonestly. Kay wondered if Lazarre could have been the lawyer who handled the Huntley property.

Realizing that Madame Le Blanc would be coming to question her soon, she sneaked back to her room. A few minutes later the woman tapped on the door.

"Come in," Kay said, preparing herself for a difficult interview.

"How are you feeling, Mary Jane?" the master's wife asked, pretending to be kind.

"My ankle is much better, thank you."

Madame Le Blanc sat down on the edge of the bed, looking at Kay slyly.

"Mary Jane, I was thinking only this morning—you have never told us very much about yourself. Your mother, she must have been a very talented dancer, yes?"

"My mother never danced a step in her life," answered Kay truthfully.

"No?" The woman could not hide her disappointment. She hesitated a moment, then said, "You speak French very well, Mary Jane. Often I say to my husband, 'that girl must have lived abroad.'"

"Really?" asked Kay, pretending to be very flattered. "I've always wanted to go to France and live, but I've never even visted there."

Madame Le Blanc questioned the girl a little more, but Kay answered cleverly. Soon the woman went away, seemingly satisfied that Mary Jane could not be related to Trixie Rue.

All that day rehearsals went on. Considering the harshness of the teacher, Kay passed the various tests with flying colours, but long before the girls were dimissed she was tired enough to drop. She had never before put in such an exhausting day in her life and wondered how the delicate Mary Jane endured the strict training.

After dinner, Kay wrote another note to her mother and one to her double, asking Mary Jane to come and trade places with her the following evening.

"By staying here tomorrow I'll have a chance to find more evidence against Lazarre and his sister," she thought. "Monsieur Le Blanc has kept me so busy today I've had no chance to do anything except dance."

Throughout the afternoon Madame Le Blanc had watched Kay closely, and even after rehearsal ended she scarcely allowed the girl out of her sight. Kay couldn't get away from her long enough to slip away from the house and hide her letters by the road.

At last, in desperation, she convinced Elaine to take the message, telling the romantic girl that it was a secret note to Hal Peterson. Whether or not the letter was picked up she had no way of finding out since Madame Le Blanc never stopped watching her. As Kay was going to her room, the woman blocked the stairway.

"Oh, Mary Jane, just a moment, please."

Kay got ready for more questions.

"I know that your last name is Barton," Madame Le Blanc said, "but when we were talking this morning you did not tell me who your mother was before she married. Could she have been related to the Huntleys?"

"The Huntleys? Weren't they the people who owned this house?"

"Yes, I think so," the woman admitted reluctantly.

"They had a lot of money, didn't they?" Kay went on, thoroughly enjoying the uncomfortable look on the woman's face. "I heard they died abroad leaving a rather large fortune, but there was some mix-up about it. Did you ever find out who received the money?"

"I—I wouldn't know anything about that."

"Since you rent the house I thought you might have heard. You do rent it, don't you?"

"Why, yes—yes, of course," the woman stammered.

She lowered her eyes and retreated hastily to the kitchen. Kay smiled as she went on up to her room. She had put an end to the questioning, and had even added to her information. From Madame Le Blanc's guilty manner it was easy to guess that the Huntley house was being used rent free. Probably it was being given by the dishonest Lazarre.

After everyone had gone to bed, Kay tiptoed downstairs once more. Entering the den, she closed and locked the door. Satisfied that she would not be disturbed, she switched on the light and turned her attention to the desk.

She spent the next two hours going through papers and letters belonging to Monsieur Le Blanc and his wife. It was tedious work, because almost everything had to do with the dance performance.

At last her patience was rewarded. In the waste paper basket she found a torn letter written by Lazarre to his sister. In it, the dishonest lawyer admitted that he had cheated Trixie Rue and her daughter out of the Huntley estate! He had substituted a fake will for the one originally entrusted to him.

"This is all I need," Kay thought triumphantly as she put the letter in her pocket. "It should be enough to convict Lazarre and show that his sister made use of the stolen funds."

Rearranging everything as she had found it, the excited girl sneaked back quietly to her room. Tumbling into bed, she slept soundly until awakened by Madame Le Blanc at seven o'clock. Throughout the day Kay was kept busy, but by this time she was familiar enough with the dance routine, so that rehearsals were not as exhausting as before.

The evening passed very slowly. Kay went to her attic bedroom at eight o'clock and turned out the light but she did not undress. By nine the entire house was dark.

Kay was beginning to worry that Mary Jane would not come when she heard creaking steps. She tiptoed to the door.

"Who is it?" she asked in a whisper.

There was no answer, but suddenly Mary Jane grasped her hand.

"You did receive my note!" Kay exclaimed in relief.

"Yes, your mother sent Ronald Earle to get it. He brought me here tonight and is waiting in the car. How did everything work out, Kay?"

"Monsieur Le Blanc seemed satisfied with my dancing. He decided that I could be in the show—or rather, that you may be in it. How is your ankle, Mary Jane?"

"Much better. See, I walk without limping now. The doctor gave me permission to dance again if I am very careful."

"You'll get along all right then," said Kay. "Monsieur Le Blanc worked us especially hard yesterday and today, and said we could have part of the day off tomorrow. Anyway, I doubt he'll be here much longer."

"What do you mean?"

"I can't tell you now, but you'll find out soon," Kay answered mysteriously. "I think I'll have some very good news for you!"

"A wonderful thing has happened to me already," Mary Jane confessed shyly. "I met Hal Peterson, and we've fixed up everything. He says he doesn't mind waiting for me, no matter how long it will be."

"I'm so glad," declared Kay with a relieved sigh. "If I had been the cause of breaking up your friendship I never could have forgiven myself. You didn't tell him about the mix-up?"

"No, and he never suspected! Some time I may tell him, but not for a while at least."

"You hold the fort here until you hear from me," Kay said hurriedly as she prepared to leave. "I'd better go meet Ronald now, and I have a lot of work ahead."

"I'm very grateful for everything you have done."

"I hope everything turns out the way I plan," Kay answered nervously. "Oh, yes, one warning. Don't let the cleaning woman see the mole on your neck. She thinks you had it removed! Another thing, Madame Le Blanc suspects you may be Mary Jane Rue and she has learned your mother is in Brantwood."

"Then it won't be safe for me to remain here!"

"I doubt that she'll bother you with questions for a while. She isn't certain, and before she can find out anything the whole mystery should be solved!"

Leaving Mary Jane to wonder about this remark, Kay squeezed her double's hand in farewell and stole down the stairway. She let herself out of the dark house and ran to the road. Ronald's car was parked a short distance from the mansion. As he opened the door for her, he looked intently into her face.

"Is this Mary Jane or Kay?" he asked.

"Can't you tell, Ronald?"

"Well, you look so much like Mary Jane, I wonder myself. All this double business is getting me confused."

"It's been pretty strange for me too," she replied with a laugh. "But right now I am sitting on top of the world!"

"That means you've solved the mystery?"

"I think so. While I was at the Huntley house I found evidence which proves that Lazarre, Madame Le Blanc's brother, defrauded Mary Jane and her mother. They were entitled to the entire Huntley fortune, but Lazarre took the money for himself while saying he had turned it over to charities named in a fake will."

"Does Mary Jane know the truth?"

"Not yet, Ronald. I thought I wouldn't tell her until I'm sure that the money will go to Trixie Rue."

"Are both Monsieur Le Blanc and his wife in on the plot?" Ronald asked.

"As far as I know, Monsieur Le Blanc took no active part. He did allow his wife to use stolen funds in promoting their show."

"All Brantwood will be amazed when this story gets out!" exclaimed Ronald. "Chris Eaton has led everyone to believe that the Le Blancs are great society people."

Kay smiled as she thought about how the Eatons would receive the news, then she became serious again. She was confronted with many legal problems which were too difficult for her to solve without the help of a lawyer.

"If only Bill were home," she said. "There are so many questions I need to ask him before talking with the police."

"Your own auto accident case will be coming up in court," Ronald remarked thoughtfully.

"I have a little evidence, but not enough," replied Kay, frowning. "Of course I could throw all the blame upon Mary Jane, but I don't like to do that, because Mr Craken would try to force her to pay a lot of money if she receives her inheritance. I'm sure he is one of those men who use innocent people. They fake accidents and force people to pay heavy damages rather than go to court. Lazarre may be involved, but that won't be easy to prove."

When the couple arrived at the Tracey home, Ronald and Kay noticed another car in the driveway.

"That looks like Bill's car!" Kay shouted.

The two ran up the front steps into the house. There was the young lawyer in the dining room, eating a big dinner. He jumped up and hugged Kay.

"Thank goodness, you're home again, Bill!" she cried with relief. "Where have you been all this time? Why didn't you get in touch with us?"

"One question at a time, please," he laughed, turning to shake hands with Ronald. "I thought you knew I had gone away to do a bit of sleuthing."

"We suspected it but we weren't sure. A lot has happened here since you went away, Bill. Has Mother told you about the car accident?"

"Yes, she was just telling the story when you got here."

"I've been accused of wrecking another car and I wasn't even in an accident!" Kay said indignantly. "The case is being brought to trial too!"

"Very interesting."

"Interesting! It would be terrible if you weren't here to help. But now that you're home my worries are over. You can tell Mr Craken and that firm of crooked lawyers a thing or two!"

Bill Tracey smiled and shook his head.

"Don't tell me you think I should pay three thousand dollars to those men!" Kay said in astonishment. "I was depending upon you to defend me."

"I will defend you, Kay," Bill answered quietly. "But there is no way for you to avoid standing trial."

25

Kay Faces Trial

"Bill, you sound like you're familiar with the case!" Kay exclaimed, rather shocked by his statement. "I haven't even told you the facts yet."

"I already know something about it," he replied. "As I've just explained to your mother, I left Brantwood to gather evidence against a group of con-men who have preyed upon people likely to settle automobile damage suits out of court. Now I come home to learn that you have been a victim of the same group of men!"

"Did Mother show you the letter I received from Duster and Trout?"

"Yes, and from evidence in my possession I am sure the firm is working with Mr Craken. The man has been involved in accidents of a similar nature before this. Unfortunately I don't have enough proof to get a conviction."

"I have a piece of paper which may help you." Kay remembered suddenly. "I found it in a taxicab and forgot about it until this moment. Wait, I'll get it."

She ran upstairs, returning in a moment with the list of names and addresses bearing the notations "W," "M," "P."

"Does this mean anything?" she inquired.

"I should say it does! This is Craken's handwriting—I have other samples of it!"

"My name is on the paper," pointed out Kay. "Do you suppose it could be a list of prospective victims?"

"That's exactly what it is. I recognize several of these names—persons who already have paid large claims."

"I wonder what the letter 'W,' 'M,' 'P' mean? You notice there is an 'M' after mine."

"It stands for medium," explained Bill. "Wealthy, medium, poor. You were singled out as a victim having about an average amount of money."

Kay told Bill about the other evidence which she had gathered, then said that it might not be necessary for her to stand trial after all.

"On the contrary, it is more important than ever," corrected Bill. "I want to get a conviction against these men, and you will be my most valuable witness. It's funny, while I went away to gather facts, my most vital evidence was right here at home."

As both Kay and the young lawyer had long stories to tell, it was well after midnight before they had pieced together the various clues. Realizing the significance of her testimony in court, Kay agreed to go through with the trial.

In the morning Kay took her cousin to Mrs Cary's cottage, intending to have him talk with Trixie Rue. They found the old lady very upset. She told them that during the night her patient had disappeared.

"I don't know what made Trixie run away, unless she was afraid of that man who came here," Mrs Cary sobbed. "She didn't leave a note or anything."

"You say a man came here?" Bill asked quickly.

"Early last night, Mr Tracey. He was a foreigner. I heard Trixie call him Lazarre and she seemed to be afraid of him."

"Lazarre!" cried Kay. "Then that explains everything. He probably threatened her, so she ran away, thinking he might send her to jail."

"Do you have any idea where the woman might have gone?" Bill asked Mrs Cary.

"Not the slightest."

This was disturbing, but the Traceys could do nothing about it at the moment.

"We have other work to do now," said the lawyer. "Our first task will be to capture Lazarre and to bring about the arrest of Madame Le Blanc and her husband."

All that day Kay and Bill Tracey worked with the police, presenting their evidence and tracing down additional facts required for an iron-clad case. By nightfall a squad of plain clothes men descended upon the Huntley mansion where not only the Le Blancs but Lazarre as well were captured.

Kay took Mary Jane home with her, and told her about her mother's disappearance. She tried to calm the girl down by promising that as soon as the Craken-Lazarre trial was over she would devote all her time to locating the missing woman.

Bill was not mistaken in believing that Kay would prove to be his most valuable witness. Taking the stand in her own defence, she said what Bill had told her to say, pleading innocent to the charge of damaging another car, and even shedding a few tears for the benefit of the jury. Satisfied that the girl could offer no defence, the lawyers, Duster and Trout, brought forth their own dishonest witnesses who swore to untrue statements.

Bill enjoyed the situation tremendously. At the right time he brought in his own evidence. He introduced Mary Jane, whose appearance stunned the courtroom. Then came Doctor Brown, the private detective who had guarded the Tracey home, and Joe. The latter had come forward to reveal that he had seen Kay taking a walk at the hour of the accident.

Everyone was relieved when the verdict was announced. Neither Kay nor Mary Jane would have to pay damages. The dishonest lawyers, Joe Craken, and the witnesses who had lied, were held on criminal charges. Hal Peterson, another victim of the group, was cleared. He had been threatened many times by Mr Craken, who was trying to make him pay damages for a fake accident.

Kay was even more excited when she learned that Lazarre had signed a confession, not only admitting a connection with Joe Craken's dishonest schemes, but acknowledging he had deprived Trixie Rue and Mary Jane of the Huntley fortune. He revealed he had led the older woman to believe she was wanted by police on an old charge involving her business partner, while actually she had been cleared of it long ago.

Lazarre still had a lot of the Huntley fortune, but he agreed to return the money to the rightful heirs before beginning a prison sentence. The Le Blancs disappeared from Brantwood.

Kay still had to locate Trixie Rue, and the task was not an easy one. Advertisements in the local newspapers failed to attract the woman's attention. Apparently she had no knowledge of the fortune which awaited her.

Kay thought that sooner or later the former dancer would return to the Huntley estate. Often she and Mary Jane went to the sunken garden to watch and wait. One evening as they sat on a bench, they were startled to see a white-robed figure come out of the gazebo and dance gracefully around the garden. Mary Jane jumped up and called out excitedly, "Mother! Mother!"

The graceful figure stopped. The white robe slipped to the ground. Slowly Trixie Rue moved toward the girls, while her daughter ran to her, throwing her arms about her.

"We've looked everywhere for you," she cried. "Oh, Mother, we'll never have to worry again!"

At first Trixie Rue could not believe what had happened and it took a long time for the girls to convince her of the truth. As they led her back to the waiting car she murmured, "It seems to me as if I am walking in a dream, and that any moment I may awaken. Yet I know it must be real, for you are with me again, Mary Jane."

"Why did you return to dance in the garden, Mother?"

"I came back to the Huntley mansion hoping to find you. I have never been able to forget my love for dancing. One evening long ago I found a white robe in the gazebo. It had been left there by the Le Blancs who often danced in the garden. I used to put it on and dance in the moonlight."

"I saw you several times," revealed Kay. "One night I heard a man singing."

"Monsieur Le Blanc often used the robe," explained Trixie Rue. "He would dance while he sang."

A day of rest and relaxation at the Tracey home revived Trixie Rue. Then she and her daughter moved into the Huntley home which now belonged to them.

A new dance director was assigned to take charge of the girls for the show for which Le Blanc had been rehearsing. Mary Jane took a great deal of pleasure in teaching Kay new dance steps. The girls worked out a funny number which delighted everyone who saw it.

"I wish we could give the dance at the charity show," Kay said impulsively. "It might convince people to come."

"Well, why not?" demanded her double. "We could call it a mystery number—a dance by Kay Tracey and her double!"

The idea appealed to Miss Grover, so posters went out immediately advertising the new attraction. To Chris Eaton's irritation public interest grew to such a point that every ticket soon was sold. Many people who had intended to go to the movie sponsored by the Eatons decided to attend the benefit for the Children's Home.

On the night of the performance, Chris, overcome by curiosity couldn't stay away. She slipped into the back of the auditorium, hoping no one would see her and suffered intensely when Kay and Mary Jane were the hit of the show. When it was over, Wendy and Betty Worth went to the dressing room to congratulate their friends and report that nearly two hundred dollars had been taken in.

"Everyone is saying that you are responsible for the success, Kay," Betty said happily.

"But that isn't true," protested Kay, smiling at Mary Jane. "My double deserves half the credit. She worked even harder than I did to create the dance."

"'Double, double, toil and trouble,'" quoted Wendy gaily, "'Fire burn and cauldron bubble—'"

"Toil and trouble, yes," agreed Kay, laughing, "but every bit of it has been worthwhile. The show was a success, Mary Jane has a fortune, and the future is bright! Could anyone ask for a better conclusion?"